CHRONONAUT 4

RICHARD HAMILTON

Copyright © 2023 Richard Hamilton.

All rights reserved. No part of this book may be reproduced, stored, or transmitted by any means—whether auditory, graphic, mechanical, or electronic—without written permission of both publisher and author, except in the case of brief excerpts used in critical articles and reviews. Unauthorized reproduction of any part of this work is illegal and is punishable by law.

ISBN: 979-8-89031-706-3 (sc)
ISBN: 979-8-89031-707-0 (hc)
ISBN: 979-8-89031-708-7 (e)

Because of the dynamic nature of the Internet, any web addresses or links contained in this book may have changed since publication and may no longer be valid. The views expressed in this work are solely those of the author and do not necessarily reflect the views of the publisher, and the publisher hereby disclaims any responsibility for them.

One Galleria Blvd., Suite 1900, Metairie, LA 70001
(504) 702-6708

THE BELL RINGER

SADIE LONG MUSHROOM HUNTER

Her head hurts. The humidity made it hard to breathe. She tried to sit up but hit her head. Her finger was tied she tried to pull the cord off it and heard a distant bell. She screamed and fainted.

Fifteen-year-old Sadie trudged to the edge of the woods. She hunted for mushrooms to bring back to the tavern where she worked since her parents were killed by Indians. Her mother trained her to tell the difference between poison and safe specimens.

Sadie was shy and always searched at dusk with Shadow her pet raven. The people of her town had gone through the witch trials and didn't roam about at night. They were afraid of the old burial ground and the seventeenth-century graves. They had bells with strings that extended through the soil and tied to the buried coffin dweller's dead, stiff fingers.

That practice occurred in the days after the grave of Dr. Moore was dug up and reburied in the higher ground due to the river flooding. By law, he was identified by relatives before reburial. There were scrape marks and broken fingernails. That indicated the Doctor was buried alive. In the second half of the eighteenth century, the blood was drained from the deceased.

Sadie's favorite mushroom and hardest to find was the town favorite, the Black Trumpet. Her second favorite was the green phantom species that glowed in the dark. The town's townspeople would *only* eat mushrooms picked by her.

She discovered a group of Trumpets hidden in the river runoffs down by the cemetery. She walked by the stone hut, where the cemetery custodian, Roger, lived. She was surprised he and his friend Robert weren't there drunk. They usually were on Friday nights.

She was startled by a squawk from a pine tree. She saw the raven, Shadow. He peered down at her. She chuckled and took a piece of chicken from her apron pocket. The giant bird swooped down and landed on her shoulder. He tipped his head and eyed the morsel. The raven grabbed the meat and flew off into the woods.

Sadie chuckled and turned back to the river runoff. She followed the ravine for a quarter mile and found a group of young Trumpets sticking out of some oak leaves. She took half of them and continued down the ravine.

She was jolted by a woman's scream from the Nashua River's distant covered bridge. It was followed by the echo of running steps dying in the forest. There was a full moon. She hid in the trees as she headed to investigate. The raven reappeared and dropped a piece of blue glass into her apron. She whispered, "Why, thank you." He always rewarded her for his bit of meat.

Sadie got within eyesight of the bridge. She scanned the area and saw quietness. A few bats flickered through the air, and a distant owl hooted. She approached the bridge. There were three pairs of footprints. One set was right down the middle of the dirt road. The others flirted with the river's edge and the overhang of oak trees.

She figured two people followed a woman. She tossed a small stone onto the roof of the bridge and got no reaction. The raven landed on her shoulder, and she almost fainted. The bird flew through the covered bridge and waited for her on a boulder by the exit. Sadie sighed and walked through.

She was alarmed to see two drag marks that led to the river's edge. She found a woman's shoe on the bank, but no sign of the owner. She heard noises from the woods and retreated. Two silhouettes appeared. One walked into the water and pulled up a woman by the hair. He yanked a shiny yellow chain from her neck and dropped her.

Sadie gasped. Two heads shot up and stared in her direction. She ran up the hill followed at a distance by two men. The woods were thick and blocked all the light. She moved away and heard the two men in the distance swear, as they ran into the trees. She took the long route back to the inn, confident that she lost the men.

She was sure Roger was one of the voices, and the other his friend, Roberwas t.

She woke up early the next morning. She stoked the stove and hearth in the tavern. She heard someone try to open the locked door and leave. A few minutes later she heard the constable's voice and the door rattle. "Open the door, Sadie."

She hurried to open it. Constable Smith chuckled. "Sorry, I could use some coffee. The rain was cold."

She stuttered. "It will take a few minutes to heat up, Sam. I just put it on." He noticed her nervous hands.

He looked out the window. "So, do you still pick mushrooms after supper at the inn?"

She spoke without looking up. "Yes, I do. I searched for Black Trumpets at dusk last night. I walked by the cemetery and the river runoff. I heard a woman scream, and footsteps." She paused and peered up at his solemn face. "I snuck down towards the noises and found no one there. The full moon allowed me to see drag marks on the dirt road going through the bridge down to the river's edge."

A surprised Sam wrote the details down. "Is that all?"

Sadie shuddered. "I heard a noise in the woods and hid. I saw two silhouettes. One walked into the water and pulled up a woman by the hair. He yanked a shiny chain from her neck and dropped her. I gasped, and two figures chased me through the woods. They ran into trees and swore. They never got near me. I think one of the voices was Roger, but I am not sure. Who was the dead woman?"

Sam chuckled. "I'm afraid I only asked about mushrooms. I knew nothing of this. Are you sure you didn't dream it.?"

She frowned and shook her head. "Well, there was the new shoe I found. I tossed it in the bushes when I heard the two men."

Sam asked. "Did you recognize anyone, maybe Robert?"

She shook her head. "No, I couldn't see."

Sam frowned. "I saw him try to open your door. Maybe one of them saw you?"

Sadie stared. "No, they couldn't see me. I'm sure, but they know I searched for mushrooms at dusk on Fridays."

Sam sighed. "I will investigate. You should not walk alone until this is over. If Roger or Robert questions, you tell them you found a shoe near the river and were afraid some poor woman had drowned. Don't show any fear."

Robert came through the door and was shocked to see Sam. He walked over to the hearth to get warm. He made no eye contact. Sadie decided to confuse him. "So, I found a new woman's shoe by the bridge this morning. Maybe someone dropped it. I tossed it in the bushes, where I could find it if a woman searched for it."

Sam knew what she was up to. "Well, it floated down the river from Concord. I doubt anyone will ask for it. I'll go look around when the rain stops. I'll buy you supper later, Sadie." He waved and left.

Robert chuckled. "I think he liked you. What about a shoe?"

Sadie laughed. "I found a shoe while I was looking for wild carrots this morning."

He asked, "Why didn't you get them when you mushroomed hunted last night?"

She sighed. "I felt poorly and didn't go out. The cod made me ill." She started bacon, beans, and fish for the early morning diners. She set out maple sugar for the porridge eaters.

Roger came in and sat with Robert. Robert pushed a hot hard cider over to his friend. He told Roger what he heard and shrugged. "It must have been someone else. Sadie was sick and didn't go out for mushrooms. Sam was here with her. He would have questioned me if it were her."

They left after breakfast to look for the shoe and see if the body was still under the rocks in the water. The rain was cold and heavy. The two men moved the woman's body to the other side of the river and covered it with rocks. They couldn't find the shoe. Roger looked at the strong river current and shook his head. "We can't leave her there long. A log could push the rocks off. Tomorrow, we will bury her in the ground somewhere else."

The rain stopped. Sam and his assistant, Steve, searched around the bridge for evidence of foul play. The rain had obliterated everything. At the covered bridge, where the storm couldn't reach, there were visible drag marks. Steve found several broken branches near the water's edge. Sam surmised, "It looks like something was dragged through the bridge, and tossed in the river here, but was gone now. We will go back to town and see if anyone is missing, especially a woman."

They went back to the tavern in the afternoon. The widow of General Whitlock had missed her weekly trip to buy oats from the livery stable. Sam took a ride out to check on her. She was not there. The house had been ransacked, and her jewelry and money box had gone. Sam had found his victim. His German shepherd Penny sniffed the ground outside the home.

After five minutes Penny barked. Sam chuckled, "I guess Penny picked up a scent." The excited dog trotted, nose down towards the road. He found a new shoe in a bush. The men were surprised when the dog detoured towards the bridge and ran through it. He sniffed the shore, where Sadie said she saw the body. Sam looked down at Penny and chuckled. "That's all you got?"

The insulted dog barked at the two men. His nose went down, and his tail wagged. The dog turned in quick circles. He yipped and followed his nose to the cemetery.

Steve looked at Sam with alarm. "That's not good." The dog led them to Roger's hut. It was empty. Sam shook his head. "I wouldn't put it past those two braggarts."

Roger and Robert sat in the tavern and drank ale. They tried to figure out what to do. At the next table, a maid told the mayor there was stuffed chicken with fresh mushrooms. She assured him the mushrooms were picked by Sadie the night before. The two men looked at each other.

Sadie came out later. Roger confronted her. "You told me you didn't go out Friday night."

Sadie blushed and whispered to him, "Deacon Lane wanted to take me for a walk. The last time I went with *him* for a *walk*, he tried to tear my clothes off. I'm fifteen he is seventy. I should tell his wife, but the tavern wants his business. That was my excuse not to go with him." The men looked over at the portly deacon and chuckled.

Sam and Steve appeared a half hour later. Steve had the shoe with him. They walked around and showed the find to the various people eating dinner. Several women recognized it as one of Wendy Whitlock's new shoes. The two men finished their drinks and left before Sam got to them.

They headed to the cemetery hut to drink. Roger was shocked to see large dog tracks around the shelter. "It's either a wolf or Sam's dog Penny." The two men followed the tracks back to the river's edge. They were happy to see they were at the first location and not the other side of the river.

Robert got scared. "We got to move the dead widow before Sam checked the other side of the river." They returned to the hut to wait for darkness. Roger purchased a small keg of rum with some of the stolen money.

There was a gust of wind and a rumble. A storm approached. Roger heard the small bell on an ancient grave blow in the wind. He smiled. "We can bury her in the old deacon's grave with the bell. His relatives had all died. The town people thought it was haunted."

At dusk, they retrieved the body from the river and put it in a cart. Robert covered it with hay. A loud protest from Sadie's pet raven, Shadow shocked them. Roger whispered, "If the raven is here, Sadie might be around looking for the glowing mushrooms." Robert threw a stick at the angry bird. He missed.

They remained quiet for a few minutes but heard nothing. They pushed the cart up to the old section of the cemetery. They had a couple of drinks and removed the layer of dried, dead grass from the deacon's grave. They were spooked by the old rusty iron pipe that led down to the coffin. The leather string that was connected to the little bell hung limp. They dug the six feet down to the knotty pine coffin's top. They both avoided the pipe as much as possible.

Robert pried the lid off and was pleased to see damp bones and rotted cloth. Roger stared down into the hole. "We will throw the bones in the river and burn the clothes." Robert pocketed two silver coins that had been placed on the dead man's eyes.

The bones were loaded into an old burlap sack and dumped into the river by Robert. A loud clap of thunder made him scurry back to the open grave. Roger dropped the widow's thin body into the coffin. Roger laughed. "The old deacon must have been fat. Look at all the room that was left." Robert shivered and looked around.

Ice-cold rain spits down, and lightning hits an oak tree on the edge of the woods. Robert saw the raven ten yards left of it in a pine looking down at them. He pointed it out to Roger. "Blast, that might be Sadie's raven."

Roger stared at the trees swaying in the gusts. "Circle behind the cemetery, and see if she is there."

Robert nodded and slipped down the hill. The woods were void of light. He scanned the trees. He detected a faint green glow move towards the cemetery. He approached and got a squawk from Shadow. He sat on an ancient stump. Robert rasped, "You little loudmouth." He threw a large rock at the bird. Sadie lunged in front of Shadow. The piece of granite hit her temple. She yelped and fell on the wet pine needles.

Roger returned from the hut after he tossed the clothes on the fire in his fireplace. He saw Robert bent over Sadie. "What did you do to her?"

Robert cried. "I threw a rock at her bird and would have killed it. She jumped in front, and the rock hit her instead. I think she is dead."

Roger chuckled. "I would have killed her anyway. She might have seen us with the dead widow."

Robert sighed. "But I liked her, and I never killed anyone before."

Roger stared at him. "You can say some words when we bury her." He realized Robert was a problem.

The raven sat in a large oak tree. He watched Sadie for movement. He saw none and realized he had lost her. Roger kicked the Widow Whitlock into the hole and laughed. Robert picked up Sadie and lowered her down. Roger bashed Robert's head with the shovel, and he fell sideways into the grave.

Roger sighed and climbed down. He put Robert's face up with the widow's face down on him. Roger had to squeeze Sadie in the side, facing the other two. Roger nailed the coffin lid on and made sure the pipe and string stuck inside the coffin's lid. Roger walked down to the river and washed the blood off his hands and the shovel.

He heard an angry squawk from the raven and threw a rock at him. The rain and thunder started to increase as Roger returned to the grave and filled it in. He carefully placed the grass back. He was pleased that the cemetery looked undisturbed. He returned to his hut to get drunk and watch the thunderstorm display.

The morning was sunny. The owner of the tavern was alarmed that Sadie had not come down to stoke the fire. He sent the other girl up to Sadie's room to wake her. She ran back down and told the man she hadn't slept in her bed. Several patrons became alarmed and figured she slipped in the storm and got injured.

The rain washed away any footprints. They searched the usual places where Sadie looked for mushrooms with no luck. They checked around the cemetery and the covered bridge area. Sam found a spot under a tree where the rain hadn't penetrated. It had drag marks. A body might have been pulled out of the river. The trail ended there.

The tired group wandered back to the inn for dinner. Sam noticed Roger sat and ate alone. He and Robert were the only inn regulars who didn't help search for Sadie. Sam walked over and sat down. "You and Robert were the only ones not to help in the search."

Roger asked, "What search?"

Sam stared at him. "The search for Sadie and the Widow Whitlock."

Roger shrugged. "I didn't know."

Steve sat next to Sam. "Where is Robert?"

Roger shrugged. "He said he was going to visit his sister Mary, she lived in Concord."

A man came in the door, and the raven flew in. It always landed on his perch, but this time he lit on Roger's table and started squawking at him. Roger turned red and reached for a knife. Sam grabbed his arm, and fellow constable, Steve, put his hand on his flintlock.

Sam stared at Roger. "Shadow is angry with you. I suppose you have no idea why?"

Roger regained his composure. He tapped on my window for a handout. I threw a cup of water at him." The two men didn't believe a word.

Sadie woke. She coughed and reached for her head. Her hand hit the coffin lid. She screamed and felt the two bodies next to her. One was warm, but the other cold. She cried and pounded on the lid till she was exhausted. She felt the string and pulled it several times but heard no ring. She resigned herself to the fact that she would die there.

She heard her breaths. She listened for an hour. She noticed the air got humid. She thought she could detect a distant scraping sound. She smiled. "Someone knew I was here."

It got louder but sounded like it came from under her. "Maybe they buried us upside down." She lifted her arm and dropped it. No, the coffin faced up.

The scrape got loud, and there was a growl. The wooden side away from Sadie splintered open, and something grabbed the widow and dragged her out of the coffin. Five minutes later, Robert's body was removed. A few seconds later, something stuck its head back in and sniffed the air. Sadie screamed. There was a soft hiss and silence.

The air became drier, and the temperature was cooler. Sadie knew she would die if she stayed where she was. She could hear the tunnel start to collapse. Sadie had to get out now. She felt the jagged edges of the broken coffin and crawled out of the hole. After several feet, the yellow clay soil behind her collapsed and sealed her fate. She could only follow the tilted tunnel.

There was a blue glow that increased in intensity. It made no sense to Sadie, but she continued the crawl. The ground got slippery, and she heard a dull rumble.

She started to slide downward. She thought of all the things she would never get to do. There was a bright blue light, and she was in the air. She was out of the tunnel. She fell fifty feet into the icy water. She was in a river. The water was violet. She struggled to remain afloat. The speed of the stream picked up dramatically, and she heard a loud roar that muffled her screams.

Sadie was surprised to see the water slow down. She glanced at the shoreline and was shocked to see giant blue men with small pointed horns. They growled and screeched at her from the shore. The growl, the same as the coffin invader.

She realized the roar was from a waterfall. She swam as fast as she could for the shoreline. She bumped into a young blue child, panicked in the water. She grabbed him and swam for the shore. The current was too strong, and they went over the falls together. She hit the bottom with her feet and pushed upwards hard. She and her blue friend broke the surface. It took all of her strength to pull away from the suction caused by the falling water. She made it to shore and fainted from the effort

Sadie opened her eyes and was shocked to see an eight-foot-tall, blue woman. She pushed a small clay plate towards her. It contained a woman's hand. She screamed, and the woman shrugged and tore off the ring finger and offered it. Sadie shook her head. This pleased the woman, who stuck the whole hand in her mouth as she left. She yelped and pulled a small ring from her mouth and tossed it away.

The young boy, whom she had rescued, brought her a bowl of berries. Sadie tasted one and nodded to him. He went back to his tribe of cannibals.

She walked down to the river's edge and drank. She hoped the purple color was not caused by blood. She was surprised to be grabbed by two giants. They had a ritual. A medicine man with a mask drew something onto her forehead. She fell asleep on some moss under a tree.

Meanwhile, Sam smiled at Steve. "Let's take Penny for a walk along the river." Roger's face turned white. Shadow's squawked in approval. He flew out an open window to the oak tree by the entrance. Sam got a handkerchief from Sadie's room. He and Steve walked the quarter mile to his house. His horse Peggy saw him and whinnied. Penny, who slept near the young horse, sat up and barked. He saw the handkerchief, and his tail wagged.

Sam chuckled as his shepherd jumped up and down with glee. Shadow landed on the corral gate and stared at the young dog. Sam whistled, and Penny trotted over. He buried his nose in the perfumed hanky.

They walked back to the inn. Roger watched them from the window. The shepherd caught the scent near the entrance but lost it twenty feet down the road. Shadow squawked, and the group followed him. Roger swore to himself. "I should have killed that blasted crow."

He rushed out the door and headed to his hut to get his pistol. The raven led them to the edge of the woods, where Sadie was hurt. The rain had washed away all the blood. Steve shrugged. "I don't see anything here." Sam noticed the daylight dying. "Huh, there must be an eclipse. We better wait until it passes. It is probably a partial."

Nope. It was a full eclipse. Steve laughed. "I can't even see my hands." The Raven cawed. The men and dog all turned towards the sound. Sam squinted, "I think I see a green glow."

Steve shook his head. "I don't see it." A glowing green mushroom flew through the air towards him. It stopped right in front of his feet, and Shadow cawed. Steve swore at him.

Sam chuckled. "I guess Shadow understood English." The eclipse passed. The dog ran over to the spot that glowed and sniffed in quick circles. The men found several picked mushrooms.

Sam looked at the limp fungi. "Sadie said they could only be found a hundred yards east of the cemetery. The dog led them to the tree with drag marks near the base. The dog barked to indicate her scent. Roger watched from the woods and swore.

Sam shook his head. They followed the drag marks but lost them at the edge of the woods. They were headed towards the cemetery. Penny lost the scent when they passed the last tree. The bird flew towards the hut. Roger hurried to get there first. He hid his pistol under his sweater.

Sam and Steve came in ten minutes later. Roger managed to drink two mugs of rum. Sam scanned the inside. He noticed several pieces of

Robert's clothes. Roger saw him. "He left his clothes here after he took a swim to clean up before he left to visit his sister."

Steve laughed. "It was pretty cold for a bath." Roger was shocked to hear a bell ring. He tried to ignore it, but it was heard by Sam and Steve.

Sam chuckled. "The owner of the inn knew Robert well. He has no relatives."

The bell rings got louder. It unnerved Roger. He shrugged. "That's what he told me." He glanced out towards the cemetery. A clatter of hoofs rumbled by them. Roger laughed. "The wind gusts ring the bells." Sam kept his eyes on Roger and his hand on his pistol.

Steve looked out the window, "There is no wind, and the sky is blue. Penny was outside. He barked and hopped around. "Let's go out and see what he is excited about. You lead the way, Roger?"

Roger walked out toward the jumping dog. He hesitated when he heard the bell ring. Roger was shocked to see Shadow, the raven, yank the bell's string. He swore and pulled out his pistol. Roger shot at the bird but hit the gravestone breaking off the top corner.

Shadow flew over to the undamaged section of the grave. Both men had guns on Roger, who dropped his pistol. "I hate that blackbird. So, what if I tried to shoot him? He is just a stupid bird. He snorted. "Is there a law that protects crows?"

Steve picked up Roger's weapon. "It is a raven… and a pet." Penny sniffed the ground around the other stones on the hill. He returned to the broken stone area. Sam watched fear build in Roger's face. The raven hopped down to the ground and picked at the sod. Roger grabbed a shovel and tried to crush the bird.

Steve laid him out with a punch to his jaw. The raven squawked and picked at the grass. A curious Sam nudged it with his foot. The grass was loose. He looked down at Roger. "Pick up the shovel and dig, Roger." He backed up out of shovel range and trained his pistol on Roger. Roger didn't move. Sam lifted his eyebrows and pointed at the shovel with the weapon.

Roger grabbed the shovel to use as a weapon. Steve backed up and chuckled. "I declare, you sure have an aversion to work… *dig*." Roger started. He pushed the loose sections of grass out of the way. He peeked at the two men with guns. Steve got angry. "Dig faster." The pace quickened, and so did his eye movements.

Roger got down to the coffin. The excited dog caught Sadie's scent and jumped into the hole. Roger jumped out with the shovel. Sam chuckled and jumped down to get his dog. Roger raised the shovel to kill Sam. Steve shot him in the chest. Sam shook his head. "I guess we know what is in the coffin."

Roger slumped on the dug-up loam. "Robert and I killed the widow. Sadie saw us hide her. Robert hit her with a rock. He headed to tell you, so I killed the moron. They are all in the coffin." He lifted his head and looked at the bird. "It's your bloody fault. He coughed once and died.

Sam pried the lid off the coffin. He found it empty. Steve looked at the hole in the side. Yellow clay blocked the outside of the coffin hole. "What happened here? Maybe they were never in the coffin."

Sam found a woman's sandal and Robert's tricorn hat. He discovered the bracelet he gave Sadie for her fifteenth birthday and a bitten-off man's thumb. He scrambled out of the hole. "No, they were here all right. We can't tell anyone about this. We will bury Roger in the coffin and say he must have fled.

Sam and Steve tossed Roger in the hole. They nailed the top on with a rock. They filled the void in and rearranged the grass chunks to look like they had been untouched for years. They didn't know two eyes watched them bury Roger.

The constables walked back to the cemetery hut, to do a proper search. They found two bags, with twenty gold coins. They must have stolen the coins from Widow Whitmore. The coins had an unknown language written on them. Sam looked perplexed. "The widow and general never traveled far. I wonder where they got the strange coins.

Maybe they were British sympathizers. I'll send one coin to Harvard University to see what they think."

They found several stolen articles that belonged to people who Roger said moved to other towns. They found his barrel of rum. It was almost empty. They poured it into two steins to finish it off.

Steve chuckled. "I think we earned a drink, after all the stuff that happened. I don't think Roger would mind." They touched and emptied them in five minutes. They fell asleep. A gun barrel jabbed their chests and woke them.

The major gave an order. "Tie Sam and Steve up." His self-importance was palatable. He resented orders from Sam, the law in town. "You are arrested for the murders of Wendy, Sadie, Robert, and of course, Roger." We have an eyewitness Constable, Widow Harwood."

Sam laughed. She is blind as a bat. "Roger confessed to the three murders. He tried to kill me with a shovel and Steve was forced to shoot him. Now Major, leave here and let me do the job the *Governor* appointed *me* to do."

The Major smiled. "Sorry, I declared martial law. We will dig up the bodies, have a trial, and hang you two before supper." He made a speech to the townspeople. They didn't like it. There was a lot of pushback. A rider was sent to Concord for help. The major had the road blocked, and the man was arrested.

The major stuck out his chest and spoke to the town members. "I am going out to dig up the bodies. You will all come, I insist. I'll prove to you people I am right. Then, I'll have a trial and hang both murderers." His men had muskets pointed at the crowd.

Everyone followed the soldiers to the old section of the cemetery. There was a crude wooden table from the hut set out with two chairs. The major paraded out Widow Harwood and seated her. "Tell us what you saw."

The major held her hand. "Tell us what you saw, Mrs. Harwood." He smiled the people pushed closer to hear.

She gave a frightened look at the crowd. "I wasn't close, so I couldn't see who they were, just silhouettes."

The major squeezed her hand, hard. She yelped. "You hurt my hand. Do you want me to lie? What kind of a trial is this, Major? These men are constables. You can't judge them."

He got angry. "This is a military trial. The rules are different. We kept our eyes on all of you, civilians. We finally caught two killers, and they will get what they deserve. This trial is for three murders."

He looked over at the grave his men were dug up. He heard them hit wood. The sergeant yelled. "We hit it, Major."

He nodded to two of his men, who threw ropes over a tree branch. He smiled. "The body of Roger should satisfy you." The men removed the lid of the coffin and just stood there. The major was getting angry. "Well? Take the body out of the hole. We can get this over before supper."

The nervous man sighed. "But it is empty, Major. The coffin contains a bag. The body might have been removed by someone." The soldier handed up the bag. "It is heavy, sir, and there is a large hole in the side of the coffin."

The major looked in the bag and smiled. He peered down into the hole. "Who put this money in there, and what did he want with the body?" He sighed. "Let them go... *for now*. We will find the body. Tomorrow, I'll send four men down the hole to find Roger and the others." He poured the gold on the table for his men to see. "I'll ask for volunteers." His men smiled.

Sam and Steve found out their rider had been arrested. They went back to the tavern to eat and talk to the town leaders. They didn't like the pompous major and figured they would get rid of him for good.

The major had only forty men under his command. He was in town to keep an eye on British sympathizers and smugglers. His commission as a major was bought by his uncle, the largest smuggler in the commonwealth.

FALL IN THE VIOLET. DIVE IN THE BLUE

Sam and Steve wanted to keep an eye on the major. The mayor brought seventy armed volunteers to the gravesite in case someone decided to arrest Sam or Steve. Sam had Penny with them. He was surprised when Shadow landed on his shoulder. The major had his four men ready to go in the hole.

Their greed numbed their fear. The soldiers had two pistols and a sword, each. They jumped into the grave and fought each other to be the first through the hole then scurried inside. It became wide and headed downward. The men noticed a blue glow that got brighter as they descended.

Meanwhile, a low-pitched drum woke Sadie up. All the blue beings headed to the river. They were armed with rocks and spears. She followed them at a distance. They came to the opening she had fallen out of and waited. The drum stopped. She noticed two beings further upstream. There was a crude dam with purple logs in the slots. They pulled out three, and a torrent of water tripled the force of the river.

Four soldiers screamed and fell from the sky. They swam towards the shore but saw the blue giants. They tried to fire their pistols but had wet powder. The spears and rocks kept them away from the shore.

They didn't notice the roar until it was too late. The soldiers would be an early lunch. Sadie walked back to the bottom of the falls. Several of the giants had spears with ropes tied to them. They laughed and competed to see who could snag the most bodies.

The major waited for his men. He sipped his flask of rum. A thick blue fog rushed out of the grave. There was scratching on wood and then a loud growl. Penny growled too. The hair on his back stood up. He hesitated for a second and jumped into the blue fog.

Sam yelled. "Penny. No." He checked his pistol and jumped in, followed by Steve.

The blue fog was sucked back into the hole. The major saw four bags on the coffin. The major looked inside. Each had twenty large gold coins. The major looked at the troops. "Sergeant Burbank, take your squad and catch them. They tried to escape. There will be a reward for their return."

Burbank and his six men went down into the grave. The major pointed to the hole with his pistol. The men went in with pistols drawn. The major wondered how many gold coins the dog would be worth.

Sadie noticed the river slowed. They must have replaced the logs. A frail voice spoke to her. "They only take out the logs when food comes down the cave, my dear. I am Dr. Moore. *You* saved the leader's son. You see, they cannot swim, their bodies are too dense. That, my dear, is why you are alive. The tattoo is from the grateful leader. It gives you a great power. I don't know what it could be."

Sadie was surprised to hear the drum again. A minute later, the river surged. The beings were back at the river, armed with spears and rocks. She was shocked to see a dog falling from the hole followed by two men.

She recognized Penny, the German shepherd. She grabbed the boy and pointed at the dog and men bobbing in the river. She thrust a spear and shook her head *no*. The boy ran to the leader and spoke to him.

Sadie jumped into the river to try and save the dog before he went over the falls. Sam and Steve were a hundred yards behind. Sadie struggled to catch up, but she couldn't gain any ground. The water lowered, and Penny and Sadie plodded safely to shore. Sam and Steve tread water. They kept their distance from the blue giants.

The dog recognized Sadie and bounded over for hugs. The leader gestured to the men to come ashore. They hesitated. The leader yelled to his guards on the shoreline, and they dropped their weapons. They backed up and permitted the two men to swim in. They were relieved to see Sadie and Penny.

They were surrounded by blue giants. One squeezed Steve's arms and legs. He pushed the giant's hands away. Some others started the same routine on Sam. He asked Sadie what they were doing. She gave him a sly laugh.

A frail voice answered him. "To see if you need to be fattened up." The two shocked men looked back at an old man with a cane. He had on a gold collar. He bowed. "My name is Dr. Moore."

Sam looked shocked. "But that was not possible. You died in seventeen forty-six."

The doctor chuckled, "These people have strange powers. Their water gave the power of life, to some people." He showed a similar figure they had painted on his head. "Sadie was given a power different from mine."

Steve looked him over. "He looks like the painting of the doctor in the library. It may be him, and we could all be dead."

Sam frowned. "What do you mean by, *fatten up*?"

The Dr. pointed to a female, chewing on a human arm. "We fatten up our pigs and cattle before we eat them. They do too."

The drum beat. The river water sped up. Six soldiers screamed and fell from the sky. The blue beings lined the shore again. The leader glanced at Sadie and her friends. Sam spoke to the Dr. "Tell the leader, these are bad men and have swords and pistols." He did. The leader grinned and uttered a command.

One of the soldiers got close to the shore but was rebuffed by a spear. He fired his pistol and had dry powder. It hit a blue giant in the shoulder. He screeched and dropped his spear. Two nearby spears hit the soldier's chest. He drifted motionless toward the falls.

The wounded blue giant was brought to Dr. Moore. He laid him down on a mossy spot. He eyed the giant warily. Sam and Steve walked over to see if he needed help. The Dr. gave him some fermented berry juice. "A couple buckets of this wine should knock him out, so I can get the ball out. You two might be needed to keep him still."

The nearby giant men nudged each other and laughed. They sat in the shade. They expected a show. Sam looked over at the doctor, and he blushed. "Well, *once in a while* the patients move around a little." The males under the tree grinned at the two men.

Sam smiled at them. "Well, at least they are not going to eat us."

Steve laughed. "At least until the operation is over… or they run out of tasty soldiers."

An hour passed and the operation began. Dr. Moore poured wine into the wound to clean it off. "You two better grab him, just in case." The group of blue men chuckled.

The Dr. made his first cut. Sam and Steve screamed as they flew twenty feet in the air and landed in the river. The blue men roared. The two men struggled out of the water. Steve's pants fell, and he landed face-first in the mud. The men exploded with laughter. He blushed.

Dr. Moore smiled. "Hurry, the wine will wear off. The opening is wide enough, but now I have to extract the ball."

Steve laughed. "You are not serious, Doctor?"

The smirk said it all. The blue men were shocked the two men returned to help the doctor. They chuckled and nodded. They waved their friends over to watch.

The bullet was taken out, and the pair flew thirty feet out in the stream. The hysterical blue men fished them out of the water. Dr. Moore snickered. "No more rides, gentlemen. I stitched him up while you were playing in the water."

The blue men patted them on the back. Sadie had tears from laughing. Penny licked the skin off them. There was a large party with dismembered soldiers. Sadie and her friends ate berries. Penny didn't like fruit. Sam talked to Dr. Moore. "How come you are not dead, sir?"

He laughed. "These beings are here on vacation. They live in a world without time. I live there now. I don't age. I just come here to fix them up if they get injured. The water can restore life, but if they are injured here, they can't make repairs themselves. That is my payment for restoration to life. I can leave if I jump off the black cliff into the blue mist. I have to trust their story since there is only blue fog as far as the eye can see. They say it is a barrier to other places and the jumper will survive… *somewhere*."

The next morning there was a lot of activity. Sadie asked the doctor what was going on. "We leave for our world. They give you your lives. You can't go back to the cave you came through. It will age you, and you will die. Find another way if you can. If the giant comet arrives and you're still here, you will die. That is why the blue beings are ready to leave." They shook hands and just faded away. The only noise was the wind as it roamed through the berry bushes.

The major saw blue fog drift out of the grave. There was a loud roar, and the blue mist swished back down the hole. The major smiled at the bags of gold on the coffin and greedily looked over at the soldiers. They recognized the look and backed away from the hole.

The mayor stared at the major. "What is going on here and where is this gold from?"

The major stepped in front of the mayor, nose to nose. "I am conducting a murder investigation here. I am in charge, not you, mayor."

The angry mayor got in his face. "You are in charge only until the governor restores Sam and Steve. They figured you would block the roads, so two men went through the forest. The governor will have you arrested for this. You probably have two days to escape. I would leave now if I were you."

The major took two men to bury the gold. His two men did not return alive. The fact was not lost on the rest of his soldiers. Their two bodies were put in the grave.

The mayor saw enough, "Arrest them." The major and soldiers opened fire on the people. The mayor fell to the ground dead.

The angry people aimed their guns at the soldiers. They threw their hands up. The assistant mayor looked at the hole. "You men will pay for the deaths with gold."

He pointed at the major. "*You* will lead." The major tried to run but was grabbed and pushed into the grave. His men were pushed into line behind him. He got on his knees and begged for his life. The man behind him pulled him up by his hair. "At least die like a man." He kicked him into the hole.

Penny's ears went up. She barked at the hole in the air and growled. Sam looked at Steve. "We have company. We have to remove the logs from the dam. We had no weapons to fight with."

They got out three large logs. They headed downstream to the falls. Sam looked back and saw about twenty men fall through the air. Sadie watched and shook her head. "They didn't drop their muskets. They will reload with dry powder."

Steve looked up in the sky. "Look, the comet and the soldiers made it to shore."

Sam nodded. "The doctor said if we follow the stream, it will turn sharply at the black cliff." They trotted to get out of musket range. They heard a shot and increased their pace. They got into sight of the river's sharp turn. The black cliff took their breath away. Another shot rang out followed by a loud roar.

They glanced back and saw a transparent wave coming towards them. The river rocks and soldiers rose into the sky. They saw the cliff edge and the blue fog. There was no choice. Penny wanted to go back, but Sam grabbed him. Steve grabbed Sadie's hand and jumped. Their screams were swallowed by the thirsty fog.

Sadie's head bounced back and forth in a wagon. Sunshine hit her eyes; it hurt too. A scruffy man who smelled of tequila was lifting her skirt with a gun barrel. He grinned, and she kicked him low. He screamed and slapped her face.

The man who was driving the wagon shot him in the chest. Two men on horseback laughed. The tall one leaned over the dead body. "Well, he told ya not to touch Abby." His friend scanned the horizon for the marshal and posse. "There ain't no dust, Stone."

The woman's head throbbed. She felt a bandage. She didn't recognize the name Abby or any of the men with her, though the leader looked familiar. She saw the chests in the wagon that had Wells Fargo stenciled in white. One of the men on a horse tossed a rope around the dead man's leg and yanked him out of the wagon.

His friend gave him a surprised look. He shrugged. "Why should the horses carry a dead man? They had trouble enough with the two wagons of gold coin."

She didn't like the leader. He was Spanish and had a large mustache. She respected the two men on horseback. The other wagon driver was an Indian, she didn't trust him. Stone wiped the sweat from his hat and looked at a map. "We should find the shiny rock tomorrow."

They found a small stream and a cliff overhang to hide the wagons. They made a fire to heat some beans and bacon. They couldn't shoot game since they were in Indian Territory. Stone scouted the area for escape routes.

He could see for ten miles. He saw vultures circling on the rear horizon. He smiled, "They found our dead friend. The men ate and shared a bottle of redeye. Stone looked at the young woman. "Can't you remember anything, Abby?"

She shook her head and stared at the ground. Stone nodded. "You got a crease in your head by a bullet during the robbery. That was three days ago. We got three thousand gold double eagles."

"We have thirty miles to the sacred Apache area. They won't follow us in there. It has a volcanic glass outcrop called Black Rock. The Indians call it Apache Tears. Beyond that point, there are canyons everywhere. We will hide out for a week and let the law stop the search for us. I will have to mark the trail well, or we will never find it again."

Abby was dumbfounded. "I helped you *rob* someone?"

Stone smiled. "Well, a wife helps her husband, right?"

His two men saw Abby's face and laughed. The red-haired man shook his head. "He's joshing you, Abby."

Stone looked at her and frowned. "You don't have to look so relieved." His men hooted at him. Abby explored the area around the cliff. She found a lot of water-worn, smooth black stones with white flakes, that she could see through. She filled her pockets with them.

In the next afternoon, they passed Black Rock. They headed into the canyons. Stone chipped weather-worn sandstone walls, as they traveled deeper into the sacred area. The chipped stones exposed a bright red surface, countering the dull light brown patina of the old canyon walls. Abby thought that was a bad idea and dropped the pieces of obsidian, whenever there was a choice of directions.

Abby looked down at the wagon tracks. "Don't you think we should wipe out the tracks, Stone?"

He snorted. "The tracks are only on the loose sand. The wind and rain will wipe them out. Just rest and leave the figurine to the men folk." The men all howled with laughter. She gave them a sarcastic smile and took a nap.

She woke to gunshots. Stone had shot his three men in their backs as they slept. He chuckled. "It looks like you will have to drive the first wagon, sweetheart." Stone tossed the dead men's guns in the second wagon and pushed the bodies into a small arroyo.

She swallowed her rage and slid onto the first wagon's seat. She managed to drop her rocks whenever they made a turn. Stone laughed. "The rocks will do *you* no good." He tied his horse to the back of his wagon. He took the saddles off his men's horses and switched out the tired wagon horses. He slapped their rears and they ran off in a northerly direction. The men's gear was tossed onto the bodies.

The posse heard the echoing shots ahead. The deputy guessed, "About five miles, I reckon. No rush, they will run out of water, and the horses will tire from the weight of the gold." A couple of the men nodded.

Several hours later, Stone noticed a hard-to-see cave ahead. "Drive the wagon into the back of the cave, sweetheart." Abby knew her end had arrived. Stone parked his wagon next to hers. He watched her as he removed the horses.

Abby knew what was next. She edged herself closer to the wagon with the guns. Stone watched her, with amusement. "You're a smart girl." He shot her, and she fell headfirst into the sand. He cut a branch and went out to scatter three horses and scrub the wagon tracks back from the last two forks.

Abby groaned and crawled to the case of dynamite. She put in a ten-second fuse and waited for Stone to return. Abby knew he had removed the guns from the wagon. Abby could hear him outside. She lit the fuse and banged a board against the cashbox.

He ran in and laughed. "I guess I should practice my aim." He shot her again, and she died with a smile. He became alarmed and scanned the cave. He smelled the fuse and ran.

A wall of sedimentary rock smothered the cave entrance. He was thrown ten feet into the air. He struggled to his horse and crawled on. He had a broken leg and a concussion. He passed out and fell off. He woke and screamed with pain. It was night and got cold. He started a fire, with sagebrush twigs.

There was distant thunder. It headed his way. Soon the ice-cold rain pelted down. He sat against an old dead pine. He smiled to himself because the storm would wipe out all the wagon tracks. He laughed, "I am the only one alive who knew where the gold was."

He heard the click of a pistol, and several men laughed. A man on a palomino spoke. "Hey, gringo, you have a pretty horse. You have a pretty gun too. Why don't you let me see it, *yes*?"

Stone stood up, "Sorry, I have a broken leg." His hand started to drop slowly towards his pretty gun. The Mexican's friends laughed. That alarmed Stone. He moved his hand away.

One of the men removed his gun. The Mexican bandit got off his horse. "So, what you do way out here?"

Stone shrugged. "I prospect a little."

The Mexican laughed. "Well, you ought to know, twelve claim jumpers follow you. I thought they were after me for the reward." He raised Stone's gun. "Does it shoot straight?"

Stone laughed. "It worked fine… for *me*."

The Mexican looked surprised. "So, you say. I maybe can't shoot your gun, gringo?" He aimed the gun at Stone. "You have any money, maybe?"

A man nudged Stone and held out his hat. Stone emptied his pockets. The man felt his pockets and looked at the leader. The man put a knife to his neck. Stone placed two twenty-dollar gold pieces in his hat.

The man brought the gold to his leader. He read the dates and got excited. "Poncho, this gold she is from the sixty-thousand-dollar Wells Fargo robbery. So where is my gold, gringo?"

Stone lied. "I won those two coins in a poker game."

The leader chuckled. "You know, I think your gun she shoots to the left." He looked in Stone's hat and took out two fifty centavo silver coins. "Let's try your gun." He nodded to his man with the hat, who moved Stone back to fifty feet.

He handed Stone a coin. He held the coin straight out to the side. He laughed and shook his head. He squeezed the coin with a folded elbow next to the shoulder. Stone swallowed hard and nodded.

The leader aimed, but his hand shook. One of his men handed him a bottle of tequila. He gulped down a third of the bottle. He asked Stone about the gold.

He shook his head. "I won that gold in a poker game, I told you." The leader's shake was worse, but he took the shot. The coin bounced off a tree behind them. A Mexican with a cheek scar showed Stone the coin. It was hit on the edge. He laughed at Stones' expression, with four yellow teeth.

The coin was brought to the Poncho. He shook his head. "I can't tell which of the four directions the coin was held. We do again." Mr. Toothless handed Stone the second coin. "Make sure it has the date at the bottom. So, where is the gold?"

A defiant Stone looked at the coin and held it out as before. The leader motioned with the gun to move it towards his chest. Stone played stupid. The leader gulped down the rest of the bottle. He tossed it in the air and shot it without looking.

The Mexican took the coin and slowly moved it towards Stone's heart. Stone filled with terror. "I told you, I won the coins."

The man stopped when the coin was in front of Stone's heart.

Poncho chuckled. "I believe you, Yankee." The coin flew through the air as Stone fell to the sand, dead.

A voice yelled down to the men. "Drop your guns." The Mexican bandits fired at the voice. A deputy fell to the ground and groaned.

The posse opened up on them. It was over in five seconds. The sheriff swore. "I told you just wing them. Now they can't tell us where the gold is."

An angry man yelled, "But they killed Jake. It ain't our gold, sheriff."

Meanwhile, fourteen-year-old Scott sat halfway up the grassy hill with the three girls. "Okay, you found my baseball, and you say you expect a reward?" The girls giggled. The tall redhead nodded. She produced a bottle from her backpack and smirked.

He laughed. "What are you going to do with *that*?" She spun it on the grass. It pointed to the blonde Debby. She squealed and planted a kiss on his lips, and he blushed. The game continued for ten minutes.

Scott mumbled. "You guys can keep the ball." A large bird landed on an old gravestone and watched them. The girls didn't like being watched. Scott tossed a pine cone at the bird.

The bird cawed at him. He chuckled. "Five more minutes and I have to go eat supper." There was a ringing noise. The three girls looked up the hill. Debby ducked down. She looked accusingly at her redheaded friend Sally. "It is probably your stupid, little brother."

The ring continued, and the frightened girls snuck down the slippery hill to the road. A curious Scott walked uphill toward the ring. He saw the huge raven sitting on an old gravestone. There was a bell with a string attached going into the ground. The string was in the bird's beak.

He chuckled. "You little troublemaker, your bell ring scared the girls away." He tossed a small stick at the stone, and the bird retreated to an oak tree on the edge of the cemetery.

He was shocked to hear the bell ring again. There was no wind. He held the string, and the noise stopped. He felt a tug from the ground. He yelped and released it. The bell rang again.

The bell ring lost strength. Scott read the stone, "Deacon Lane born 1699 died 1788." He read about him in the library when he wrote a history homework assignment. The bird was back cawing at him. The bell ring became more intense. His neck hair rose. He swallowed hard and trotted home.

Scott's favorite supper sat on the table, baked stuffed chicken. His mother expected it to disappear, in about two minutes. A jittery Scott just played with his food. His mother and father looked at each other. His twelve-year-old sister had a big smile on her face. "He is probably tired from Debby, Sally, and Mona kissing him for an hour."

Scott blushed. "They found my autographed baseball in the field, and would only give it back if I played ah, spin the bottle." His father smirked. His mother looked angry. He mumbled. "It was only ten minutes, Mom. They got scared away when the bell next to a gravestone, rang."

His sister Carol nodded. "Yes, that *was* strange. I heard it too. There was no wind. You should have seen how fast Scott bailed out of there." He frowned at her, and she laughed with glee.

Their house was a half mile from the cemetery. Both his parents had decided to repeat the 'birds and bees' monologue from two years earlier. His parents laughed off the bell story. Scott retreated to his room to sulk, and do homework.

He went to bed at ten. A thunderstorm woke him up at two. His parents had convinced him the bell was imagined. The storm and the wind ended. He heard distant rings. He opened his eyes and decided he was awake. He pulled the pillow over his ears, but his mind wandered back up the hill.

He sighed. "Dad was right; girls were trouble." He put on a pair of shorts and sneakers. He could still hear the bell. He ambled towards the cemetery. He hoped it would stop. It didn't. There was a heavy fog from the storm. It blanketed the lower gravestones. He walked into a large one and yelped. His shin bled.

He thought he heard a laugh, maybe he had lost it. The bell got his attention back. He walked up the hill and shined a flashlight on the clapper. It rang with urgency. He walked around the stone and saw nothing. He shined his light in the trees. He expected to see the smart-aleck raven. Nope.

He stood in front of the grave and looked back down the hill. A large bird landed on his shoulder. A startled Scott screamed and fell backward over a gravestone. His feet stuck up in the air like a TV's rabbit ears. The raven hopped on his foot and looked down at him and squawked. He heard the hysterical laughter of his sister.

He frowned. "What are you doing here?"

She smiled. "I figured you'd meet your three kissy-face girlfriends." She chuckled, "Seriously, I heard the bell." Scott was surprised to get licked in the face, by his German shepherd, Winston. He was still on his back, with his feet draped over the stone. The raven waved his wings but remained on Scott's foot. His father tried to look mad. "Exactly what are you two turkeys doing up here?"

Carol looked innocent. "I heard Scott go out. I followed him, so when he got in trouble *again,* I could run to get you."

Scott frowned at her. "I heard the bell ring, *again*. I thought someone needed help. Who would ring a bell at two in the morning?" He was shocked to hear the bell again. His sister laughed. The raven was on the ground, pulling the string.

Their father looked at the stars and shook his head. "You two will be on laundry duty, for two weeks." He motioned down the hill. Scott thought of a protest but knew better.

The raven flew down and landed on Carol's shoulder. He saw the sparkling earring and grabbed for it. Carol yelled and covered her ear. "No, you don't, you little crook. They cost me two dollars."

Her father laughed at the raven. "It will cost you two dollars. You have two dollars?" The bird squawked. "I thought not." He flew into the night.

The father didn't tell his wife about the night's escapades. The next school day consisted of Scott's avoidance of the three girls. Luckily, none had classes with him. His last activity was biology. The teacher was a spinster named Miss Provine. She was surprised when Scott stayed after class to talk to her since he had the highest class average.

He looked down at his feet. "Miss Provine, how long could someone live if they were buried alive in a coffin?"

She chuckled. "Read Edgar Allan Poe, did we?"

Scott was surprised. "I thought he was a poet?"

She stared at him for a minute. "Is this unknown person alone in the coffin?" He gave her an uncomfortable shrug. "Let's see, a coffin is usually seven feet. A person uses about 30 liters of air an hour. I would say alone 5 hours and with a friend *alive* 2 hours due to displacement and usage. If the friend were dead, just the volume displacement, so I would say 3 hours. Why do you ask?"

Scott sighed. "You wouldn't believe me. My father thinks I am crazy. If a person can only live a few hours, he's probably right and it is too late." She watched him leave. She remembered about the mayor of Maynard's lost teenage daughter. She knew it was her duty to call the police. Maybe they would put her picture in the paper.

Carol sat in the backyard and read, "Watchers" for her book report. Her mother weeded the window box. She was startled when a hefty raven landed on the box edge. The bird cawed and peered at her stud earrings. He saw Carol and hopped onto the picnic table.

Her mother watched with fascination as the bird hopped over to her. It cawed and bent its neck to see her earrings. Carol laughed and turned sideways. "Yes, they are the same ones."

Her mother looked surprised. "You know this bird?"

Carol looked guilty. "Yes, I met him in the cemetery one evening. He tried to pull my earring off my ear." She chastised the bird, "I told you it will cost you two dollars." The bird cawed and flew off.

Ten minutes later the mother looked up. "Your little friend is back."

The bird landed next to Carol. He had a large piece of blue glass that was smoothed by the ocean. He dropped it and pulled at her earring. Carol yelped and covered her ear. "No. I want money, you little crook, *coin of the realm*." He grabbed his blue sea glass and flew off. Her mother watched him disappear into the trees.

They thought they saw the last of him, but he returned ten minutes later. He landed beside Carol placed a large coin on the table and pushed it towards her with his beak. Her mother squinted at the coin from the flower box. "That looks like gold." The bird tipped his head and pushed it closer to Carol.

She picked it up. "Boy, it is heavy." She nodded to the excited bird. She took the earrings off and held them out. The bird walked over and took them. The happy bird cawed and flew off with his prizes.

Her mother looked at the coin. "My god, it is an old American 1871 twenty-dollar gold piece. It looks new. It is probably worth several thousand dollars." Carol ran into the house to get another pair of earrings.

SPINNING A GRUESOME TALE

The mother was surprised to see her husband pull into the yard with Scott, followed by a police cruiser. She ran outside. "Is Scott hurt?"

Her husband snorted. "No, dear. The police just think he buried a girl alive in a coffin, you know, the usual kid stuff. They're here to interview him."

Scott smiled. "The police took me out of study hall in freaking handcuffs, right in front of everyone. Maybe I should have agreed to go to the dance with Captain Clinton's daughter."

The two policemen laughed. They went inside. They put a recorder on the kitchen table and read Scott his rights. The sergeant smiled. "Do you know Sara Gould? She is the missing girl from Maynard."

Scott looked surprised. "No, I generally stay within my town, when I build a harem. I get it. Miss Provine put you up to this because I asked about coffins."

The sergeant chuckled. "Well, Scott, how often does a student ask a teacher, *how long can a person survive being buried alive in a coffin*? You can see why we might be curious."

Scott chuckled. "I figured a biology teacher would be more likely to know the answer than a math teacher, even though she is a nut case."

The sergeant snorted. "Okay, the big question, why ask it?"

Scott blushed. "I played baseball in the field and lost my Fenway Park foul ball that I caught last year. Some girls found it, but would only give it back if I played their little game with them in the cemetery." He blushed, "Ah, tag."

Carol snickered. "Don't you mean spin the bottle?"

The police laughed. "Then what happened?"

Scott glared at his sister. "The girls and I heard a bell ring and they became spooked. They raced out of the cemetery."

Carol chuckled. "Maybe they realized their mistake."

Scott grunted. "I followed the sound to the oldest part of the cemetery. There was a grave with a bell with a cord that ran down an iron pipe into the coffin. I saw it ring and grabbed the cord. I could feel something pull on it. I believe my dear sister heard it too. There was no wind. I feared someone was buried alive, maybe that girl that was lost."

Scott showed them the gravestone and bell. There were no signs of disturbed ground. The giant raven landed on the stone and scared the crap out of the officers. He recognized Carol and hopped onto her shoulder. He peered at her new earrings.

Everyone stared at her. She blushed. "The Raven is my friend." Her father noticed she didn't wear her favorite earrings. His eyebrows rose, and she looked down at her feet. He chuckled.

The sergeant regained his poise. "We will need the names of the girls, to check out your story." Carol grinned. The sergeant was annoyed when he heard his daughter's name. He chuckled. "Just realize that someday you will have a driver's license, son."

Scott relaxed. "I'm sure the other two girls talked her into going, sir. She only liked seniors, with motorcycles and leather jackets. I was only a junior, and my dirt bike didn't qualify."

The police left. The second officer was teasing the sergeant with the names of all the local senior bikers who had been arrested. The sergeant smirked. He thought he might have been hasty with Scott.

Scott's father heard the conversation of the men and chuckled. He walked back into the house and saw his wife's laptop open to a page on American gold coins. She had clicked on an 1871 twenty-dollar gold piece. He had a vague idea about what had happened.

Carol saw him and chuckled. She opened the fridge and got him a Miller beer. His wife walked in and saw the look on his face. "You figured it out. I knew it was better to marry for brains, rather than good looks."

Scott came through the door. He laughed. "Good one, Mom." They filled the men in on what had happened.

His father chuckled. "Your friend was back at the cemetery. He scared the police to death. He eyed Carol's new earrings. He looked like he might plan to get them."

Carol blushed. "I liked the attention. It is pretty cool to have a wild bird as a friend."

The sergeant sat at his desk. He filled out the report of his interview with Scott. The officer, who went with him, tried to keep a straight face. "Hey, Sarge, they found the Maynard girl. She is alive. She eloped with her secret, biker boyfriend. He has three outstanding warrants. He jumped bail to get married. Isn't love grand?"

The three girls verified Scott's story. The sergeant gave his daughter the choice of no phone for two hours or grounded for a week. The week would go fast.

The story spreads. The next school day a lot of girls milled around in the hall. Scott opened his locker, and a hundred bottles fell on the floor. Many shattered. The girls exploded with laughter.

The janitor knew about it. He chuckled and handed Scott a broom, dustpan, and barrel on wheels. "Get used to it son." He finally headed to class and saw the poster. It offered kisses for one dollar.

The girls from the cemetery waited outside the room and laughed at him. He chucked and wrote on the bottom of the poster in red ink and entered the classroom. The girls rushed over to read it. It listed their names and a price of three dollars for them. They blushed and got angry. The other girls read it and giggled.

A local TV station picked up the story and listed it below, *Things you don't hear every day*. The school calmed down, but when the kids got off the school bus, they were inundated by reporters. An aggressive woman shoved a microphone in Scott's face. "Sir, you and several girls witnessed the bell ring on Deacon Lane's grave?"

Carol chimed in. "I did too."

Scott laughed. "I saw a large bird pull the string, and it was windy from a passing thunderstorm. What, no politicians got arrested today, and Bigfoot is on vacation?"

Carol wouldn't let it rest. "But we saw it happen, more than once, and on different days with no bird or wind."

Scott grunted as reporters surrounded his excited sister. The raven landed on her shoulder and pecked at the nosy reporter. The cameras took pictures of the bird.

Scott grabbed Carol's hand and pulled her out. "It is time to go, mighty mouth." The bird remained on her shoulder. He turned back and scolded the reporters. He flew away when the pair reached the front door. Their mother had left to buy KFC for supper. It was a weekly tradition. The reporters hung around outside.

Scott looked out the window and shook his head. "Maybe you should stay inside and work on your memoirs."

Carol blushed. "Oh, that is funny, *sugar lips*." Scott cringed, and she laughed.

Far away, at a local frat party, people watched the comments by Scott and Carol and the gravebell ringing incident. They were shocked when the raven landed on Carol's shoulder. They believed the girl and decided on a road trip, to find out for themselves.

They arrived an hour later and grabbed shovels from the maintenance hut. It was ten o'clock, and no one was in the cemetery.

They found Deacon Lane's grave. They were shocked to see the bell start to ring. They dug in shifts.

Carol finished her homework and went to bed. She heard an urgent tap on her window. Her little flashlight lit up the raven. She chucked and opened her jewelry box. She removed her new earrings. She unlocked her window and the bird hopped in.

She put the jewelry on the sill. The bird looked carefully at them but squawked. The raven flew out and back. Scott watched from the doorway. "He wants you to follow him."

The pair tried to sneak out, but they were nabbed by their father. "Where do you two think you are going at ten o'clock on a school night?" Scott looked embarrassed. "Um, the raven wants us to follow him, Dad. He seemed upset. It will only take a couple of minutes." His father sighed. He got his flashlight. "This better not be a wild goose chase." The raven cawed from the backyard.

He led them to the cemetery. They could see the glow of lights on the hill. They approached and watched a bunch of drunk men and women try to dig up Deacon Lane's grave. They were about halfway there.

The bird circled above them and squawked. One man threw a bottle at him. The bird avoided it. His friend swore at him. "If you're going to throw bottles at the bird, throw empty ones, you dolt."

Scott's father called the police. It took eight patrolmen to subdue them. Two of the women were topless. The police wrapped crime tape around the site and the two well-endowed women. The students reached the coffin lid.

The next morning the police inspected the site. They were about to fill it in when the raven landed on top of the lid. He tipped his head and listened. He pecked at the top. The sergeant hopped down in the hole. He noticed the side of the coffin was broken into. He decided to open it to inspect to see why.

He made the smart-ass patrolman pry the top off. He was pleased to see the man faint. He took a picture with his phone. "Jake, Josh, drag *Mary* out of the hole." Two patrolmen hopped in the hole. Their faces turned white, and they scrambled out.

The sergeant chuckled. "Now what?" He jumped back into the hole. He saw a girl with her hands tied behind her. She looked dead. He pushed her away from the coffin hole.

There was a skeleton of a man. His hand was tied to the string. The hand jerked up and down. It rang the bell. The sergeant almost fainted. His men laughed. He swore. "Whoever pulled that bell, will walk a beat."

A man laughed. "It was the bird, sarge, I swear." The raven peered over the hole and cawed.

The sergeant chuckled. "Oh, you're hilarious. Call an ambulance, but give them only our address. Dave put up more crime scene tape further out. Set up a fifty-yard perimeter scan. Check the trees, bushes, and grass."

The ambulance arrived. The sergeant told them they found a body tied up behind a gravestone. They checked her pockets but found nothing. They thought she was dressed oddly. She had a tattoo on her forehead.

Carol stuck a mini camera in a bush pointing at the grave the night before. She watched the ambulance race by their bus on the way to school. She couldn't wait to see what was on it.

She told her friends at school about the hidden camera. She did not inform them of the location. There was a rumor that the police had found a body. The sergeant's daughter, Mona, heard it on the secondary police channel. She told her two best friends. They promised not to tell anyone.

School ended at three. Carol couldn't wait to get home and get the camera. Scott had heard rumors of a camera. He would mess with his dear sister. They arrived home. Carol ran upstairs to change her clothes. She raced back down and saw Scott look at his phone.

Scott looked serious. "Mom says to stay in the house. Some big mouth told everyone about the police arrests last night. There will be too many weirdos out."

Carol shook her head. "I think I lost my phone on the hill last night. I have to go look for it."

Scott shrugged. He picked up a baseball bat. "I go too."

She sighed, "Whatever."

Scott retraced the exact route they took the night before. He saw the tape still surrounded the gravesite area. "Huh, that's odd. They left the police tape up." Carol reached into a bush. The cube camera was gone. Scott watched Carol fish around for it. He shook his head. "It is not around here."

He chuckled when Carol threw her phone under the bush. She nodded. "Yes, I had it here last night. I used it as a light." She searched again but found no camera. She picked up her phone. "I found it."

Scott struggled not to smile. "We better get back. Mom will get home soon."

Carol sat in the backyard. The raven landed on her table. He greeted her and hopped over to check out her new earrings. He tugged on one gently. She laughed. "You can have them, for cheering me up." She took them off and held them in her palm. The raven hesitated. She held her hand closer to him. He tipped his head and looked at her face. He slipped his beak around both prizes and flew off.

She wondered what she would tell her friends. They would think she made up the story. She realized they didn't know much about her character. Ten minutes later, her friend was back. He had her square mini camera in his beak. He dropped it on the table and pushed it towards her. He cawed once and flew off.

Scott had watched from the porch. "So there was a camera." She snickered. Her brother thought she made it up. "Well, let's see if you got anything cool on that thing."

She downloaded it to her laptop. "Well, at least it's not blank.

Scott laughed. "You probably got branches blown by the wind." They watched it in silence. They saw the police remove a tied-up woman. "Look, they sent for an ambulance. Maybe the woman was alive. But wait, she was buried in a coffin for several days. She should have run out of air."

They watched the men fan out to look for clues. Carol chuckled. "I wonder why they didn't find my camera."

A patrolman's face lit up. "Sarge there is a camera in the bush." Several men ran over. The image suddenly spun sideways. The sergeant yelled. "Get that damn bird."

The picture straightened out. The police just watched the raven fly away. There were thirty seconds of darkness and several bright blue flashes of light. Ten minutes later, a full moon came out from behind the clouds. Scott chuckled. "It's a fake. The full moon is not for two more weeks."

There was a minute of darkness and movement. Then a slit of moonlight lit the area in time to see the camera drop into a chest of gold coins. Carol's earrings, some blue sea glass, and shiny black stones littered on top. They didn't recognize the terrain.

The kids showed the file to their parents. They watched with dropped jaws. Their mother sighed. "Sooner or later, someone will associate Carol with that bird."

Her husband frowned. "Copy the entire file to several thumb drives. Edit the camera's file. Erase everything after the police. We will have to find someone beyond reproach, to *accidentally* find the camera in the cemetery."

Carol chuckled. "How about Scott's three little spin-the-bottle kissy friends? I'm sure they will be back for more sugar. Mona is the sergeant's daughter. She could make it seem like a legit find, but the sergeant isn't stupid, it might not work,"

Scott blushed. "Her father hates me. I would get in trouble all over again."

Carol laughed. "Yes, that is a caveat, but he would feel relieved since you are not a biker. You are the lesser of two evils."

Scott sighed. "What I have to do for humanity."

Carol smiled. "I'll tell them you hope they will want to play again."

Scott glanced at his mother and blushed. "Why do I have to be so irresistible to women?"

His father chuckled. "You inherited that trait."

His mother snorted. "He's right. My grandfather was a cad."

Carol let Scott have the cube. "You better edit the camera file, quick. Then you'll have time to buy a nice pink bottle and some chapstick." Scott grunted.

Scott had a copy of the camera end footage. He had timed the bird from the cemetery to its final destination. It was nine minutes and fifty seconds. He looked up the flight speed of a raven. He didn't like the extensive range of thirty to sixty miles in an hour. He would use ten minutes and forty miles an hour. He rounded the distance up to seven miles.

He found a road map in his mother's glove compartment. He drew a seven-mile circle around the cemetery. He chuckled. "That is a *lot* of ground." Scott looked at the video frame by frame. There were a couple of seconds of the landscape. It was sandy, with scrub bushes and distant mountains. He looked at the circle. There was nothing like that anywhere, and then there was the full moon. He rechecked the math and upped the flight speed to fifty.

Carol was glad she planted the camera the night before. The three girls followed Carol home. They told their parents they were going to get help from Carol with their algebra homework. They saw Scott in the backyard.

They squealed and chased a surprised Scott up the cemetery hill. He fell on the camera. They started to kiss him. He screeched. "Something bit me on the back. He rolled over and picked up the cube. "What the heck is this?"

He held it right in Mona's face. She looked at it and threw it away. "Who cares what it is." She clamped her lips on Scott and fell on him.

Sally waited for her turn and picked it up. "Huh. This is a mini camera. Didn't you say your father searched for one?"

She got off Scott and pouted, "You just can't wait your turn, Sally."

Mona took it and sighed. "I *suppose* I *should* give it to my father." She walked home. The two girls waved goodbye.

Her father was a happy camper. He didn't even question what she was doing in the cemetery with her friends. He watched the video. "I wonder *why* the bird took it?" He didn't like the end. It was too tidy. He would have the lab check it out.

The girl was in a coma. Her clothes were taken to the police lab. They had found two twenty-dollar gold pieces in each shoe. All were dated 1871 and appeared to be new.

The doctor took a picture of the symbol on her forehead. He emailed a copy to the police and one to a professor of languages at Princeton. She had on a small garnet ring, primitively cut. Her core body temperature was 53 degrees Fahrenheit. It was unlikely someone could survive that low a reading.

The police found traces of blood on her clothes. They were handmade, as were her shoes. There were no traces of soap residue or deodorant on her. The lab man chuckled. "We ran the trace blood for a DNA signature. We are checking hers, for a family tree."

The next day the girl's body temperature returned to normal. She remained in a coma. The doctor was shocked by her emerald green eyes. She had a rugged, outdoorsy look. Her hands were rough from hard work. He checked her med list. She sat up and screamed. "Die, Stone." She scared the daylights out of the doctor. She fell back down in a coma.

Later, the girl woke up. She looked around. Her eyes locked on the TV, which had a Harry Potter movie on. Her eyes saw a dragon and opened wide. The TV smoked and shut off. The nurse who washed her face stared into her eyes and fainted. The girl fell asleep. The burning TV set off the fire alarm.

After a few minutes, the nurses smelled the TV. One took a towel and pulled the plug out. She opened the window and noticed the unconscious nurse on the floor. She summoned help. The doctor checked her head and found a pronounced bump. He ordered an MRI.

The faulty TV was removed, and a replacement was brought in. The doctor checked the girl. She was asleep. He looked around. "I wonder what happened here."

The MRI was negative. The nurse was awake but jittery. She talked to the doctor. "The girl opened her eyes and saw the TV. She looked at it like she had never seen one before. Harry Potter came on with a dragon scene. Her eyes opened wide at the screen, and suddenly the TV started to spark and smoke. I gasped. She turned and looked at me with those eyes. That is the last thing I can remember. Doctor, I believe she's an alien."

The TV repairman told them the TV was toast. "I never saw anything like it. Maybe it got hit by lightning. Strangely, the surge protector didn't kick."

The girl was awake but couldn't speak. The doctor figured it was from psychological terror. Hell, she *was* buried alive in a coffin. She pointed at objects, and the nurse would bring them to her to be examined. The nurse chuckled to her friend. "She never saw them before."

The doctor tried to communicate with the frightened girl. She pointed to her throat and shook her head. She wanted a pad. They gave her a ballpoint pen with it. She looked confused. The doctor pretended to write in the air.

She put the pen on the paper and was shocked to see a blue line. She inspected the bottom of the instrument and made a line on her palm. She smiled and looked back at the doctor.

He smiled. "What is your name?"

She wrote. "Sadie."

"Where are you from?"

"Gull House sir."

"What year is it?"

"1746, sir."

The doctor and nurse looked shocked. The looks frightened the girl. After they left, she drew some pictures from the memory of the Massachusetts colony."

The police lab tech reported his findings. "Part of the video might be deleted. There is usually a ripple at the end. Maybe the bird's grip did something to it, or maybe it was dropped from a height. If you told me what you looked for…"

The sergeant sighed. "I have a problem with the fact my daughter found the camera. It's too convenient." He hung up and tried to imagine, what the reason would be to erase the end of the video file. He copied the camera information to try and find the buyer. He would have his smartass patrolman search. He was too overweight and needed the exercise.

The sergeant assigned his fat patrolman, to find the buyer of the mini camera. Harry discovered they only recently came out and sold at only one store. Nine people bought them with credit cards and one person… paid in quarters.

The nine were to catch unfaithful spouses. The last was a little girl, who wanted to steal her brother's laptop password. She thought he read her emails. She was blonde about twelve and tall for her age. She called her brother *Sugar Lips*.

The patrolman remembered the sergeant was mad at his daughter for the spin-the-bottle episode. The rumor was there was only one boy. He snickered. He could bust the sergeant's cookies.

He caught the Sergeant at his desk. A lot of officers were switching shifts. He spoke loudly. "I have the information on the mini camera, sergeant. Only one store sold them. Nine people bought them to spy on their spouses. One little girl bought it to spy on her older brother. She called him *sugar lips* for some reason."

The sergeant bristled. "Good job, Harry. It's that Carol Thorburn. My daughter and her friends think her brother is a hottie. Let's visit her."

The father was home and answered the door. He chuckled. "Oh, Scott, come to the door please."

Harry let out a subdued laugh. "Sir, we would like to see your daughter, *Carol*."

He chuckled. "Carol, the police want to talk to you."

She and Scott walked to the door. A confident Carol chuckled. "Yes, I bought the cube. How did you trace it to me?"

Harry smirked. "The cashier said you bought the camera to spy on *sugar lips*." Scott gave his sister a sarcastic chuckle. She frowned. "You got the camera with the police actions on it. Why are you here?"

The sergeant smiled. "We know you erased part of it. Why?"

Scott spoke. "The raven flew away… so what?"

Harry snickered. "And landed somewhere?"

Carol countered. "Yes, landed somewhere. That is what we took off the video. That is no crime."

The sergeant smiled. "Well, we would like to see it."

The father smiled. "If you want to see it, get a court order."

Harry barked. "A girl was found buried alive. That tape might show the perpetrator to us."

Carol spoke. "It does not." She looked at her father. "It is better to show these two, than the whole world." The father nodded. He opened the wall safe and tossed the mini camera to Scott. He plugged it into the laptop and played the file. Both officers leaned forward when the bird flew off. They saw the gold when the camera was dropped.

The father sighed. "There. You can see why we deleted it. All hell would break loose if the public saw it. You would have to explain how you took a live woman out of the grave and not warned the public a madman was loose in town."

Harry spoke. "We want a copy for our files." His greedy eyes locked on the cube camera.

The sergeant shook his head. "No, we don't. He's right. There is no criminal activity there. I'd lock it up or destroy it."

The father chuckled. "I told the kids they could try and find the treasure location for a week. They will fail since there is no terrain like that near us and no mountains at all. The bird can't cover enough ground. I will overwrite the file on Monday."

Harry moaned all the way back to the station. "We could have figured it out. How hard would it be?"

The sergeant laughed. "Mr. Thorburn is no idiot. He is an MIT physicist. If the area could be found, he would have found it. Do not tell anyone about the file. I will tell the captain and the DA what we saw. That will be the end of it, trust me on that."

Harry had a stable of snitches. One was Nick the Knack. He was a safecracker. He would get the damn camera, for a kilo of coke. Harry had stashed the drug, from several "botched" raids. It seemed there were shootouts and no bad guys ever survived. "I want the camera. If there is money, you can keep it. I will be your alibi if need be.

Carol saw Scott. "I didn't like the greedy eyes on that patrolman. I'd be surprised if he didn't try to steal it. Let's put a heat-sensitive camera on the wall safe."

Scott chuckled. "Good idea. I think I ought to modify the landscape shots, just in case the moron was successful. I'll go out and find something that will get him in hot water."

Scott biked around the neighborhood. He saw the DA's mansion and twenty acres of landscape, with flowers and trees. Scott didn't like the DA. He smiled and took multiple shots and angles. Scott saw his twelve-cylinder XKE convertible. He snapped a picture, with a partial number plate. He chuckled. "I can't make it too easy."

It took Scott all afternoon to edit the file. He showed Carol what he did and how he did it. "I *want* him to steal it." They made copies of the original and the edited file. His father took the money and switched the original camera out of the safe. They put the edited one in it.

Scott kept Winston, their German shepherd, in his room for the night. The dog hogged most of the bed and snored. The cat went out earlier. She could care less about burglars. Nick arrived at two o'clock. He was gone in five minutes. Scott heard him. Winston didn't have a clue. He heard a car start, about two blocks away. Scott went downstairs with Winston. He opened the safe. Carol whispered, "Is it gone?"

Scott jumped. "Where did you come from? You scared the crap out of me. Yes, it's gone."

Carol chuckled. "I knew it. I saw it all. I locked myself in the closet and watched through the keyhole. The burglar opened the safe in less than a minute. We might as well have put it in the mailbox."

Nick copied the file to his thumbnail drive. He drove to the edge of the park and met Harry. He quizzed him. "So, what is on the camera, dude?"

Harry laughed. "It is an illegal police action, taken by the sergeant. If he is fired, I am next in line for his position. I'll be able to help you more, and of course, make us more money. He buried a young girl in an old grave, but she was found alive. She was taken to the hospital to figure out who she was.

Nick took his product and left. Harry went back to his apartment to get some sleep. Nick returned home. He tried to sleep, but couldn't. Nick had to watch the video file. He was disappointed. It seemed to be as Harry said. It didn't sound like Harry to Nick.

He looked at the video frame by frame. He had no idea what the blue flashes were. There was a lot of sand and a set of mountains in the distance. He figured possibly the memory was corrupt. One minute before the image, there was a piece of an exotic car. There were four digits of a number plate. He figured he would watch it to the end. He was glad he did.

Harry had to work but watched the file before he went in. When he had viewed it at the Thorburn's, there were distractions. Harry sipped his coffee and waited for the deleted section. He watched it with full concentration. Harry smiled to himself. Yes, he saw more identification points.

Harry showed up at the station. He seemed pretty smug to the sergeant. "Hey Harry, you won't believe it, someone broke into Thorburn's wall safe. It's kind of a coincidence, huh?"

Harry gave him a sarcastic smile. "Did he get any money?"

The sarge parried. "How did you know it was one guy? Where were you at two AM?" Several men stopped to listen.

A defensive Harry smirked. "I was home in bed."

Sarge laughed. "So, you *were* alone." Several officers snorted.

Harry grimaced. "I'm not *always* alone. Ask your wives."

Sarge chuckled. "Blown-up young boys do not count, Harry."

He grimaced. "That was funny, sergeant."

Sarge sipped his coffee. "It doesn't matter. The Thorburn girl has a video of the robbery." Harry looked shocked. "You're not on it, right, Harry?"

"Sorry to disappoint you, but I was home with my blow-up underage *girl*."

Mr. Thorburn reported the break to the police. The sergeant had an idea who was involved in the theft, his pal Harry.

The only people who knew about the complete video file were the sergeant, the captain, DA, and his fat pal Harry.

The sergeant and Harry showed up to claim the safe video. Scott had made copies just in case. Scott met them at the door with the video. "I'll take it, Sarge." Scott stared the sergeant in the eye and looked over at a thumb drive on the coffee table. The sergeant nodded. "That's fine, Harry." The sergeant came inside.

Scott looked out at Harry in the car. "Look, the idiot tried to erase the thumb drive with a magnet." He gave one of the copies to the sarge, in case Harry decided to overwrite it on a laptop. "I guess he had someone break in."

The sergeant chuckled. "I'll have to prove it."

Carol gave him a sinister smile and laughed. "Not necessarily."

The sergeant chuckled. "I don't want to know."

Nick couldn't search to get a list of cars with the same four last digits. He paid a friend to get it. The police officer was some friend. He charged Harry two hundred dollars up front and other unspecified benefits. There were three hundred names.

The two policemen got back to the station. Harry plugged in the camera. He was shocked. The video file was present. The face was hard to recognize, due to the infrared. Harry saw his snitch.

The sergeant wasn't sure. He did notice a heat signature from the keyhole of the closet. It came and went. He realized someone was in the closet, and they knew they would be robbed. He chuckled to himself. He remembered Carol's strange comment, but *not necessarily*. They had a doctored video file in the safe. He snickered. He decided to let the event play out. He felt sorry for Harry.

LANDSCAPING THE DISTRICT ATTORNEY

The sergeant had an alert flag set for anyone getting plate searches using the last four plate numbers. He was surprised to find a patrolman, in the next town, had made such a request that morning… Not as surprised as Harry.

The man was off duty and home. He stood nervously at the door. He positioned his foot so they couldn't push it open. "I have a domestic abuse case. I think the husband hired someone to beat up his wife's boyfriend. I only had the last four plate numbers."

The sergeant was impressed, this boy could think on his feet. He should have had his foot on the bedroom door. Two stoned teenage girls stumbled out. The redhead swore. "Nick said to give you two hours. If you can't do it again, we're gone. Time is money, dude."

The officer blushed and stuttered. "I got the list for Nick the Knack. I have a copy of the list if you want it." He gulped.

The sergeant tried not to laugh at Harry's red face.

Nick looked at the long list of names and shook his head. He looked over the frames again. Nick noticed the fancy bumper on the car. He copied the picture to a thumbnail. Nick drove to a friend's home, who sold stolen car parts. He smiled. "Freddy baby, I need to identify a car type by just a bumper."

A voice from under a fifty-seven Corvette barked. "A hundred bucks, Nick." An offset wrench reached out from under the car. He clicked it waiting for the cash. A hundred was snapped up. It was returned in the wrench burning. Freddy laughed. "Now give me a real one Nick." He complied. "It is an XKE roadster, probably 1966." He let out a loud fart and laughed. "*That* is for the fake "C" note, asshole."

Meanwhile, at the hospital, the doctor bought the young girl pastels and a drawing pad. He smiled at her. "Can you draw pictures to show us how you got here?" She smiled and sighed. She liked to draw. She set the pad on her knees and started scribbling. He left her alone.

Sadie was sleeping when the doctor came back in the afternoon. The first picture was of Seagull Tavern, sometimes called "Gull House" established in 1686. It showed colonial-era people. Some rode horses a few walked in buckskin outfits most wore tricorn hats.

The second picture was a man and a woman with several arrows in them. A little green-eyed girl held the woman in her lap. She cried. There were two large holes in the ground for burials and a small one for a dead pet.

The third picture showed a body being thrown into a grave. There was a chipped gravestone with a bell on a piece of pipe. A large bird sat on the headstone. A second person stood to the side of the grave with a spade. There was a tipped scarecrow in the background. They were all silhouettes backlit by a deep orange sun. The nurse shuddered. "The symbolism gives me the creeps."

The doctor completed his rounds and returned two hours later. The girl had more drawings. The first one had a coffin with a hole in the side. There was a skeletal arm. It dangled out the hole tied to a string and up to a bell. The arm belonged to a man.

The second picture was of giant blue beings in crude clothing. They were eating human hands and feet. Sadie and a well-dressed old man sat and ate berries.

The third picture was a massive rock outcrop, and the ground around was covered with scattered gold coins. A nearby rock outcrop of volcanic glass was detailed. The gold coins were 1871 twenty-dollar gold pieces. The doctor mumbled to himself. "The coins they found in her boots were 1871."

Meanwhile, Harry looked at the list. He smiled to himself. "Nick will never figure this out. Damn, I may never figure this out." He decided to look at the distinctive frames. He noticed a car with a strange bumper. He went to see his snitch, Freddy. He was still under the Corvette. "I have a car I need to be identified."

Freddy cackled. "Cost you a " C " note, Harry." He put the money in the pliers.

"It is a 1966 XKE twelve-cylinder roadster."

Harry laughed. "I didn't show you the picture."

Freddy chuckled. "Nick *already* showed me the picture."

Harry swore and dashed out. He would let Nick do the legwork. He would kill him later. First, Harry had to find the owner of the car. He looked down the list and laughed. The dear DA was his pigeon. His investigation, the year before, had cost Harry sergeant stripes. He would get the treasure and frame the DA. He figured for at the least tax evasion, and the best bribery in the upcoming murder trial of his pal, Nick.

The DA liked to sleep and look out at his perfectly manicured gardens. He heard something in the air above his backyard, with a whiny sound of small engines. A drone with a light flew back and forth across his gardens.

The drone completed its mission before the DA got his 20-gauge shotgun. Freddy had warned Nick that Harry was on his trail. Nick retrieved his drone and camera. He had another drone. It was taken from the Local police station. The police didn't know it was gone.

Nick flew the second drone loudly around the outside of the house. He got some great shots of the DA who was wearing pink silk, monogrammed underwear. He got some of his wife out of the shower topless. The DA lost it and blasted his shotgun through his bedroom screen. The drone lost two motors and tumbled to the ground. The excited DA whooped and ran outside to claim his prize.

The door slammed behind him. He was standing outside in his underwear with the drone. His wife laughed from inside. She finally let him in. He carried the drone to a light. It had a serial number. He would check it the next day.

The DA had an aide call the manufacturer to check where the drone was sent. It was one of twenty mailed to The House of Science. The store clerk remembered the serial number because it was his birthday. He laughed. "Don't you and the cops talk to each other? A fat-ass arrogant patrolman bought it for his department."

The aide smiled. There was only one fat patrolman. He had given him a fifty-dollar ticket, for driving too close to the yellow line. He skipped lunch. He couldn't wait to tell the DA.

Nick chuckled; he wasn't through with his pal, Harry. He broke into Harry's Facebook account and posted the video of the DA's shot at the drone and the subsequent lock out of his house in his pink monogrammed underwear.

The DA, Mr. Burger, came back from the court at noon. He wondered why everyone smiled at him. He had been grumpy all week.

The aide showed up at the DA's favorite restaurant. He ate with his colleagues. The aide loved this. "Sir, I found the drone was purchased by the police. The clerk remembered the serial number since it was his birthday. He told the cop that bought it, was a fat-ass arrogant prick."

The people at the table laughed at the mention of the drone. One of the lawyers showed Burger the Facebook video posted by Harry. The

DA turned crimson and decided to skip lunch. The aide skipped lunch too. The next couple of hours could be epic.

The DA called in the sergeant and police chief. He told the story of the night before. He said, "My wife jumped out of the shower and the drone filmed her. She liked it. She was proud of her breasts."

He sighed. "I shot the drone down and ran outside to retrieve it. The door slammed shut. I was locked out, *in the underwear my granddaughter gave me for my birthday.* After my wife laughed herself out, a full ten minutes later, she let me in."

He smiled. "The drone was traced, and the clerk said it was purchased by an arrogant fat ass cop. Does that ring a bell with you gentlemen? Investigate him, and I expect enough evidence, to fire his fat ass." The DA found the drone was gone from the Police Tactical Equipment Locker. It was not signed out; however, the locker entrance required a keycard to be scanned.

He had his own stable of off-the-book snitches. He had a ten-year-old computer nerd, who stole people's accounts and passwords. He was on probation. His single mother allowed the DA to talk to her son alone. The DA smiled. "I investigated your pal, Harold. I think he is dirty. You can put him in jail. He would throw your butt in jail in a New York minute." Myron grinned.

An unknown named, George sat in his hypnosis class. He wanted to make his female robbery victims not remember being robbed or worse. The instructor looked for the hands of a student, who agreed to be regressed to another life. George wanted to see what it felt like.

His hand was the only one in the air. The class clapped as he came forward. The instructor used a metronome and a backward count to get him under. He was under in two minutes.

The instructor told George he could feel no pain. He stuck a pin in his hand. He got no reaction and held it up for the class to see.

He backed George up into another life. "Go to a significant event." George started panting. "What are you doing?"

George spoke in a raspy voice. "I reloaded my gun."

The instructor asked. "What is your name?"

"My name is Stone, just Stone."

"What year is it?"

"It is 1871."

"Who is the president?"

Stone cackled. "Well, it ain't Lincoln. It is that butcher, Grant."

"So, what happened?"

George chuckled. "There was a cheater at the poker table. I killed the four men."

The instructor swallowed hard. "There were four cheaters?"

George snickered. "Of course not, but there was *one*."

"Then why did you kill four men?"

"I didn't know which man it was. The bartender saw the whole thing, so I shot him too. I grabbed a couple of bottles of rotgut and took all the money from the dead men and the poker table. The saloon cash register only had 200 dollars. Now I have left."

"So, you shot all the men in cold blood?"

"I didn't know I had a choice." The class laughed.

"That didn't bother you at all? You aren't even sure they cheated."

George snorted. "Looky here, mister, *I* cheated and didn't win any money. That was good enough for me. Besides, I needed the money, now. The bank had to pay for the miners in three days. I have to prepare for the robbery."

The class hung on every word.

"Can you go forward to the next event?"

Stone chuckled. "We robbed the bank. We got away, but the girl that held our horses got grazed in the head by a forty-five slug. We had two wagons. One wagon carried the gold and the other filled with water dynamite and supplies."

He smiled. "We will outlast the posse. There was no water this time of year. We lost the posse after a few days. We got 60,000 in gold coins. The gold had to be hidden. We used glass rock as a starting point. There is no other outcrop like it."

He chuckled. "I killed my men and forced the girl to drive the wagon through several canyons. I chipped the sandstone walls so I could find it again.

"We found a cave. I made the girl drive the wagon inside. I shot her in the back. She had figured out I was going to kill her. She had lit dynamite, to take me with her. I barely got out of the cave. She was killed, and a pile of rock sealed the entrance. Some bandits found me later, and I was killed. I told them nothing."

George's girlfriend recorded the session. She looked warily at him. "Here is the tape. I'm out of here. You murdered people."

George laughed. "So, what? I got rid of the problems. Run away, little sheep. I'm sick of you."

George, the student who got hypnotized, was found in a Chinese restaurant dumpster under a half-eaten order of General Gau's chicken. The students who killed him had no clue where the outcrop was. Google was no help.

Carol saw Harry's video on YouTube. "You're my hero, Scott." The DA had stopped the girls headed to school, with purple, green, pink, or blue dyed hair.

The sergeant was at the door. Carol laughed. "I told you he'd find out."

Scott blushed and led him to the living room. "How did you find out so fast, sir?"

The sergeant laughed. "Relax. I am the only one who knows. I watched the video with my dear pal, Harry; that is sarcasm guys. I noticed the closet keyhole had a heat signature that moved around." Carol blushed.

The sergeant smiled. "I guess we know who was in the closet. I'm glad you selected the DA. He is an arrogant little prick. So why did you pick *him*?"

Carol blushed again. "He is the one that got colored hair banned from school, three days before the prom. My brother felt bad about it." Scott gave him a copy of the true video. Scott smiled at the sergeant. "Whose body did you dig up?"

The sergeant chuckled. "If I didn't tell you, you two would find out anyway. We took out a young girl. Her hands were tied behind her." He chuckled. "She is about your age, Scott, and has a rugged beauty."

Carol looked surprised. "She was not dead?"

He smiled and nodded his head. "She is in the hospital room 214. Her name is Sadie. We are stumped, and she tells quite a story. You can visit her if you're curious. Tell them Sergeant Smith said it was okay." He handed the pair one of his cards. The girl grabbed it. Scott wasn't curious. He chuckled to himself. *The boy is smart.*

The doctor worried Sadie might never talk again. He noticed a bird watching her from outside her window. The bird squawked. The girl was asleep. She slept a lot. Maybe she was concussed. An MRI isn't perfect.

The doctor felt animals might work with Sadie. He figured a litter of German Shepherd puppies might do the trick. She patted them and smiled, but remained silent.

The stupid bird was back and made a racket. The girl turned towards the sound. She smiled. "Shadow, how did you get here?" The surprised doctor opened the window. The screen was screwed shut. A maintenance man was summoned and removed. The bird flew to her shoulder and accepted some pieces of her ham sandwich.

Sadie explained the pictures. The doctor thought she was crazy. He would have a staff psychiatrist evaluate her. He got ready to leave as the nurse turned on the TV. It was another Harry Potter movie with another dragon chasing Harry, Sadie sat up and gasped. The TV burst into flames and the screen went black. Sadie fell back to sleep.

The psychiatrist listened to Sadie's story. Her English was mixed with several foreign languages. She used several words he never heard before. "You said you were *boguing* in the woods?"

Sadie nodded. "Yes, for mushrooms, sir."

"And a lot of the people thought you were a *punk*?"

Sadie blushed. "Yes, but I was not." He wrote down the words in a little notebook. "That is the strangest story I ever heard." She didn't seem to know about electricity or the box that talked. She was afraid of it. She didn't understand all of the doctor's words, and he had to explain their meanings to her.

Sadie sobbed. "It is strange to me. I have the tattoo, the raven, and the 1871 gold pieces. I have a scar from Robert hitting me with a rock, and I was dug up from a buried coffin. I still don't believe any of this."

The technician checked the TV. It was toast. "It must have been hit by lightning *again*."

The psychiatrist looked at Sadie and slowly shook his head. "No, not lightning. It was sunny out." He thought she had psychic abilities and a high IQ.

The psychiatrist talked to the doctor. "She is brilliant but has no idea what common objects are or their function. She uses words not in use since the eighteenth century. Her story is outrageous, but the clues point to it being true. I believe she possesses psychokinetic abilities. She fascinates me."

The doctor watched the tech bring a new TV. He set up a video recorder on Sadie and the TV. Sadie ignored him and had no idea what he did. She looked for her pal, the raven.

Carol decided to visit Sadie in the hospital. She entered her room with a small, gardenia plant. "Hi Sadie, my name is Carol. My brother, Scott, heard you ring the bell and eventually got you dug up."

Sadie was confused. "They told me my hands were tied behind my back. I was buried in the Deacon's grave the first time. What year is this? They won't tell me."

Carol chuckled. "It is 2014."

Sadie snorted. "It cannot be. I was born in 1735."

The TV sound was down, but Jurassic Park was on. Sadie saw it and yelped. The TV went black, and the odor of melting plastic filled the room. The nurse opened the window, and the raven flew in. It landed on Carol's shoulder. He saw Sadie and flew over to her. Carol chuckled. "No more earrings for you."

Sadie was shocked. "You know Shadow?"

Carol laughed. "Yes, the little thief stole a set of my earrings. He paid me for them with an old gold coin. I believe I got the best of the trade."

Sadie laughed. "Shadow is honest. He always gives something in return. This gold coin, was it by chance, dated 1871?"

Carol chuckled. "Yes, it was. How did you know?"

Sadie smiled. "They found four of them in my boots. I don't know how they got there." She glanced over at the dead TV. The bird grabbed a shiny candy wrapper and flew out the window. Carol took photos of her drawings. The one with the orange sun, made the hair on her neck stand up.

In the afternoon Nick smoked the DA's motion detectors with a laser. That night, Nick hired a bunch of boys to check his backyard with metal detectors. They put flags where they got indications of metal. They glowed in the dark. An expert would decide later if any were worth the dig.

The DA couldn't sleep. He imagined pigs were in his backyard. There were also buzzing sounds. He pictured pigs hit with cattle prods.

He covered his ears with a pillow, and the noise stopped. He realized the sounds were real. He looked out the window and saw the kids. He yelled, and they scurried off. Another drone appeared and quickly scanned his entire lawn.

He ran outside with his shotgun. He stepped on some of the flags and screamed. He danced to get his feet off the points but fell backward on them. He jumped up and hobbled to the front door. He looked like a turkey with all the flags sticking out of his butt.

Nick would put the video on YouTube and Facebook. He'd use Harry's accounts. The DA had the chief put Harry on foot patrol. It was a dead area where things never happened. It had video cameras every fifty yards. He could go nowhere.

The DA placed a patrolman in his backyard. He was forced to wear a body camera. The DA's wife liked to putter in her front yard gardens and work on her tan. She barely wore a bikini. It would be a long day for the patrolman.

Nick had to get the DA away from his home. He was in a chaise lounge in his backyard. To rest and recuperate from the flag wounds, in a pair of padded underwear.

He has a light blanket to hide his condition from his nosy neighbors. He read the cases for Wednesday's court. He had his shotgun next to him. He was oblivious to the fact his chair had been treated with heat-sensitive superglue.

His wife nudged him from his nap and handed him a Long Island iced tea. His arm was stuck to the chair armrest. He tried to stand up, but his legs were also glued. The officer tried to help but got glued face down on the DA. His hysterical wife called the Fire Department. Unfortunately, the press had scanners and always monitored the police and fire department.

The firemen had to fight their way through a hundred reporters and clicking cameras. His wife was pleased that her favorite blanket was not glued to her sticky husband. She yanked it away from him and was delighted when her bikini top broke open.

The DA would be in the hospital for a few days. He got the chase unglued from his rear. His wife was home. She worked on the backyard flowers. She got shot in the butt with a tranquilizer dart.

Nick chuckled and had two of his friends carry her to the living room and duct tape her hands and feet. His expert with the metal detector could use the drone photo of the flags to check the hot spots.

He marked the possible real hits with pink spray paint. He found a couple more areas in the cellar.

They were all dug up, with no success. The wife still slept. They put her out on a chaise lounge in the backyard.

The DA was irate when he finally viewed his yard. He knew Harry had a hand in it, but he had the perfect alibi. He was angry at all the photos of him in the local paper. There was one picture of his wife, after the unfortunate bikini top incident. She didn't look that embarrassed to him.

Myron, the computer nerd, hit gold. He put everything on a thumbnail drive. The DA looked at the first three pages of fifty. He would clear Myron's record. He was so impressed he gave the kid an off-the-books part-time job. He would have an assistant go through it all the next day. Maybe he could issue a warrant before the long weekend.

Harry knew he was lucky. He was on night duty so he couldn't be blamed by the DA. The sergeant figured maybe Harry's snitch, Nick, was the culprit. If he broke in for Harry, he'd copy the video. He smiled to himself. It would serve his fat ass right.

Harry laughed when he saw the video of the DA glued to the chaise lounge. His pink girly padded underwear clashed with the dark green seat covers. Harry looked at all the holes in the backyard. He realized the video of the robbery meant they knew someone would visit them. They would have screwed with the video.

He called Nick, "I have been had, or should I say we. Someone altered the video. I have to admire the fact that they screwed with the DA. The sergeant has a copy locked in the department evidence locker. We can find the gold together after you steal the *real* video."

The raven visited Carol. She had a new pair of earrings. Scott had installed a tracking device on them. It had a two-mile range. She nudged the baubles toward the bird. This time he hesitated and hopped around. He scrutinizes them. He finally grabbed the earrings, but stopped and looked into Carol's eyes. Carol felt guilty and blushed. The bird jumped on her shoulder for a second. He took a final look and flew off.

Scott followed on his dirt bike. The bird was fifty yards ahead. The sky was ideal with no clouds. He could see the bird. He thought to himself, *this will be a piece of cake*. There were several light flickers, and the bird was gone. The tracker lost the signal. He looked around with binoculars. There was no bird.

Carol returned home. Scott couldn't help himself, "I give up; tell me everything. The bird vanished into thin air." She taped the conversation and played it for her brother. He started to talk, but nothing came out. She giggled. He stuttered. "Well, none of that gibberish could be true."

Carol enjoyed herself. "Well, what about the TV? It blew up for a *third* time, witnessed by the nurse. How could she get buried in a coffin, with the undisturbed ground? And of course, we have Shadow the raven and the gold coins."

She also drew pictures of her ordeal. "You kind of look like the constable, but let's face it, he is far more attractive."

Scott chuckled. "Oh, that was funny." He looked at the rock outcrop with all the gold coins. His face turned white. He just stared at the picture. "I know this place. I saw it before."

Nick broke in and got the video, along with a kilo of coke. Harry wasn't too thrilled until Nick gave him twenty percent of it. Harry walked a beat, and Nick attended a party with friends. They each got a hundred dollars to establish his alibi.

The two men tried to decode the landscape but got nowhere. They had specialists try to identify the area. Their video expert shrugged. "It appears to be in the western United States, but the Thorburn daughter said the raven was gone for ten minutes."

Nick chuckled. "She's a liar. There is no land like that within a thousand miles. We have to pick her up and have a nice chat."

He and his friends grabbed her as she came out of the hospital. The raven saw the grab and became agitated. One of his men threw a can at him. They moved across the road to the park and sat on a bench. It faced the hospital.

Nick smiled. "Would you like ice cream?"

She snorted. "What do you want, guys?

"The real video made no sense, nor did the statement to the police. We want the real story for say, a hundred dollars?"

The bird tapped on Sadie's window. The police nurse opened it. The bird flew to Sadie's table and squawked.

Sadie got out of bed and put on the new clothes the doctor gave her. The nurse protested briefly but started to hum and dust the room. Sadie found a way out of the hospital.

Carol chuckled and held her hand out. A bill was placed in it. She took a marker out of her purse and drew a yellow line on the bill. She nodded and put it in her wallet. Nick smirked at his friends.

She sighed. "I'll tell you the whole story." The men leaned towards her when she got to the bird. "We watched the police dig up that poor girl. The bird appeared out of nowhere and tried to steal my earring out of my ear. I didn't know what to do. I laughed and said it would cost you two dollars. The bird flew off. I never expected to see the little crook again."

She chuckled. "The bird returned the next day and tried to buy the earrings with a shiny piece of blue glass. I told him I wanted two dollars and he flew off. Ten minutes later the bird returned with a twenty-dollar gold piece. I gave him my earrings. A few days later the event was repeated. It took him ten minutes again."

The raven landed on the top of the bench and pecked at Nick.

He picked up a piece of a tree branch to push the bird away. Sadie appeared and glared at Nick. The wood dropped to the ground, and the men disappeared. Sadie looked around. "Where did the men go?"

Carol chuckled. "How would I know? You made them vanish. Wait, how did you get out here?"

"My friend, Shadow, said you were in trouble."

"How did he do that?"

"He just said, *Carol is in trouble.* Well, I *thought* he did."

The police nurse tapped her shoulder. "You are in danger out here. I can see I can't leave clothes in the closet."

The newspaper received a tip, about a girl buried alive in the cemetery. They figured if it were true, she would be in the hospital. A reporter dressed as a nurse took a picture of the girl and her drawings. She went to the cemetery and got a photo of the grave. The story got national coverage, especially since Halloween was on the horizon.

Nick and his friends found themselves in a restaurant with red hot chicken wings, "Which one of you *wing nuts* decided to eat here? I can't feel my lips."

His two men looked around. The tall one shook his head. "You must have picked it, boss. I don't even remember the drive here.

The police nurse, Harriet, heard Carol talk to Sadie. She heard her tell Sadie that her brother, Scott recognized the outcrop. Harriet was Nick's snitch in the police department. She would inform him about Scott. He would arrange to grab him. His pal Harry was in jail and couldn't make bail. Thanks to Myron the DA's case would be a slam dunk.

Nick returned to town. The nurse filled him in. "I thought you were going to grab the girl? Where did you go?"

Nick chuckled. "We got a sudden urge for red hot chicken wings. The girl had no idea about the location of the outcrop. She just knew what it looked like."

INTO THE BLUE...
SADIE WILL DO

Scott had seen the paper. Sadie looked familiar. He felt uncomfortable about that. Carol continued to try and get him to visit her. The mysterious events gave him the creeps. No way sis.

The school concluded, and Scott arrived home alone. He worked on his dirt bike. His sister was still at school. She vied for the school play lead.

Meanwhile, the hypnosis students saw the story in the paper and came to town to find out where the obsidian outcrop was and eliminate any competition for gold. They found out about Scott's possible knowledge of the structure, from the spin-the-bottle triad for two cases of beer in bottles, for their Friday night party at the cemetery

Scott finished the carburetor adjustment and readied for a test run. The raven landed on his handlebar and cawed. Scott chuckled. "Sorry, I don't wear earrings." The raven cawed louder and pecked his hand. He looked back towards the road.

Nick and two of his pals showed up at the front door. The hypnosis students were thirty seconds behind them. Several guns were shot, and a bullet shattered a patio window.

A woman called out. "He's in the backyard. Shoot low, we need him." The raven urged Scott to leave. The bird led the way. Scott just followed. He realized it was the same route that he had followed days earlier when he chased the tracker.

The bird went over the hill and vanished in a blue flash. He didn't have time to brake. A bullet hit the ground on each side of him. He gunned the bike and went airborne over the crest of the hill. He screamed all the way.

The people chased him got to the hilltop and saw his damaged bike. They could see a mile in every direction. The leader was shaken. "Where did the little prick go?" They heard a distant police car. They left their three wounded men. They would slow down the police. They scrambled to their car and sped off. Nick memorized their rental car's plate number.

The police arrested Nick and his pals. They interviewed the three hypnosis students who said they stopped to help the boy being shot at. The cops had doubts but ran their thumbprints through a scanner. They had no arrests and were released. The guns found were unregistered and matched two bullet holes in the house. A complete search was done for Scott. They discovered his crumpled dirt bike. There were no footprints at all.

Scott got up to his hands and knees. He coughed up a mouthful of sand. Scott turned to see where the shooters were. He saw only sand. Scott looked for his bike. It dawned on him that he wasn't next to the cemetery. It was the night with a full moon, but there shouldn't be one for a couple of weeks.

He saw Shadow, the raven. That helped him relax. The bird landed on his shoulder and squawked. Scott started to hyperventilate. The raven pecked him on the head. He squealed. "That hurt, dude. Where are we? What happened to the cemetery?"

Scott was cold. The bird cawed at him and walked briskly on the ground. Scott followed him for half a mile. They came to an old covered wagon. There were three skeletons with arrows in them. The bird made a noise and pecked at some sand covering a blanket.

There was a full canteen half-buried nearby. Scott took a drink. It tasted horrible, but it was water. They walked ten miles. The sun had been up an hour. The bird ducked behind a small rock and peered carefully out. Scott saw him and did the same thing.

They heard horses and wagons approach. There were a couple of men riding horses. Their clothing was from the nineteenth century. The first wagon had a wounded woman with a bandaged head. A dirty man lay behind her. He had a foot wound. Scott thought they had stumbled on a movie set. He started to stand up but got pecked by the bird.

The guy with the foot wound tried to lift the girl's dress with his gun barrel. She objected, and he slapped her. The front rider on the horse shot him in the chest. All the other men laughed. One of the horsemen threw a rope on the dead man's foot and dragged him off the wagon. Later, they rested. The girl wandered off. She was collecting glass stones. Scott looked a hundred yards west and saw a bright black rock outcrop.

Scott ducked back down. The raven pecked him. He chuckled. "Okay, *you* were right." The girl looked familiar to him, but he couldn't place her. Then he remembered his sister's photo of Sadie. He whispered to himself. "It's not possible. I must have a concussion." Shadow pecked him again. He chuckled. "I guess that means she *is* Sadie?"

Scott saw the men make camp. His mouth watered when he could smell bacon, beans, and coffee. He watched them eat and dump what was left in the fire. They poured the coffee on the fire which put it out. The girl, who had eaten earlier, returned.

They all went to sleep. The raven approached the dead fire. The bird picked up a large piece of bacon, and Scott nodded. The bird devoured the whole strip. He grabbed a bean for Scott. He chuckled. "Thanks a lot."

The group got an early start. When they got out of sight, Scott and the bird scavenged the fire site. Scott found two pieces of bacon and some beans. He held out the vegetables to Shadow. The bird gave him a quizzical stare. Scott ate the beans and a small piece of a bacon strip. He sighed and gave the rest to the bird.

The pair followed a half mile behind. Scott detected some shots and ducked down. There was some hoof clatter a half mile behind them. "Great, we have *more* people with guns." They were getting into canyon country. He caught up to the dead men. One had a half-full canteen, but there were no guns. They were shot in the back.

There was distant thunder and lightning. Scott looked around for the girl and possible shelter. Nope. The bird got agitated and pecked his ankle. "Okay, I'm coming." He got a few yards into a small canyon and heard a loud roar. A ten-foot-high wall of ice-cold water passed behind him. "Now I'm glad I gave you the bacon, Shadow."

He could hear screams behind him about a half mile away. They stopped. He heard loud taps ahead of him. He followed the sound and saw the leader chip the reddish rock every hundred feet. After two hours the man pulled a gun on the girl and ordered her into a cave. He entered with his wagon and made sure there was no back exit.

He shot the girl and went back outside to scatter the extra horses. Scott edged towards the entrance. He could see the girl move. The man walked back inside and saw the girl was alive. He also smelled the lit fuse in the dynamite. He ran out as Scott ran in. He shot Scott in the back. "Who the blazes are you? Well, you're dead now." Scott dragged Sadie behind a rock in the rear of the cave and passed out.

The raven saw it all and flew away. Stone shot at Scott again but missed. The explosion threw Stone through the air. He awoke with a broken leg and concussion. He crawled on his horse and tried to leave.

Inside the cave, Abbie saw the boy's back wound. "Are you part of the posse?" She tore a piece of petticoat and tried to stop his bleeding. Some loose rocks started falling. She leaned face up over him. She was hit several times by sliding sandstone.

There was a crack in the ceiling rock. The last thing she saw was the deep blue sky. The raven raced towards the obsidian outcrop. He flew over the top and vanished in a blue flash.

He reappeared by the river of blue beings. He landed on the perch of a Golden Eagle. She was a pet of the blue people. Shadow chattered to the bird. She flew to the leader's shoulder. Shadow helped himself to some meat from the eagle's treat dish.

Two giant blue beings with the young boy headed up a cave adjacent to the cemetery cave. They came to a rock wall. The creatures made short work of the sedimentary rock. The noise made Scott stir. He saw a female skeleton on him. He figured it was Abby.

The beings broke through the cave floor. The youngster moved the skeleton gently off Scott and placed her on the dry-rotted remains of the wagon. The two giants were busy. They dumped the gold coins into a nearby hole. They topped it with sand. Scott watched but passed out from blood loss.

One of the Giants sniffed Scott. He poked him and got no reaction. The other whispered some sounds, and the other picked him up. They returned to their cave and emerged in the blue giant realm. Dr. Moore waited.

He examined Scott. The curious raven watched him. "He had a weak pulse." The doctor was surprised to find a bullet wound. He extracted it, while Scott was still out.

Scott opened his eyes and saw a giant blue woman eating a hairy-tanned arm. He tried to stand up. Dr. Moore held him down. "Don't worry lad, you're not on the menu." Shadow landed on Scott's foot. He looked him over and chirped a couple of times.

Several young blue beings stared at him. He recognized that stare. He felt uncomfortable. The doctor chuckled. "It seems you have appealed to the young women." Scott blushed. The doctor chuckled louder. "I see you have witnessed that reaction before." Scott turned redder. The doctor smiled. He was worried about Scott's infection. One of the girls who looked at Scott also had a large rash.

In the Thorburn family, Scott was still gone. The Thorburns resisted interviews from the newspapers. It had now been a month, with no clues. Several local psychics said he was abducted by aliens. The papers had nothing, so they ran with that.

A couple of scam papers talked about a possible elopement. Carol spoke to her father about Scott. The police gave up the search. Carol questioned Sadie. She had no idea where he was, or what happened. Carol noticed the bike tracks were at the same spot where Scott said the bird had vanished into thin air. The raven had not reappeared; she thought that was a good sign.

The next day a depressed Carol sat in her backyard. She yawned and threw a frisbee for Winston. She was happy to see Shadow was back. He eyed her ruby red earrings. Her mother watched from the kitchen window as the bird flew away to the north.

Her mother came out. "You have to refuse to trade. Maybe we can find out something about Scott." Carol nodded. Ten minutes later the bird returned and she rejected the offered blue glass.

Scott rested near the doctor. He was shocked to see the raven. The bird squawked a welcome to him. He got an idea. He had found a gold piece in his shoe. He scratched *I'm ok* and his initials on it. He tied a strip of his shirt around the coin. Unfortunately, there was blood all over it. The bird grabbed it and flew off.

Carol and her mother waited half an hour. The bird finally showed up. They were shocked to see the strip of bloody shirt.

Carol cried. "It is covered with blood, mom." She took out the coin and saw the message. "*I am okay, ST.*"

The hypnotists had one of their members watch the Thorburn's home. She saw the reappearance of the large black bird that might be the same one that Scott had followed.

The woman called her friends. They laughed at her. She watched with binoculars. The woman viewed the activity and reported it. "The bird returned with a parcel. All the Thorburns appear jubilant. It must contain a message from their son."

Carol tied a small strip around the earrings and gave them to the bird. Shadow flew off with his prize. He returned to the cave and found his small chest of treasures. He dropped the earrings on top of the coins. He was irritated by the strip of the shirt. He tried to remove it but failed. He cawed in anger.

He picked it up and flew back to the blue being's world. He saw Scott and flew down to his shoulder. The blue girls were in awe.

The bird pushed the rings towards Scott's hand. He picked up the bundle. He saw his piece of shirt. It said *we got it, Carol*. He saw the impressed girls. He couldn't help himself. He held one on each forefinger. The bird cawed and took them.

A few days later, the infections were worse. It turned out the infected girl was the leader's granddaughter. Dr. Moore told Scott he had no way to stop the rash. The blue leader was worried about his granddaughter.

The doctor quizzed Scott. "You said you are from the future. Do you have cures for infections? Sulfur doesn't help, and that was all I had."

Scott nodded. "Well, we have penicillin. It might help." He looked around. "But we are here, wherever *here* is."

The doctor watched Shadow try to mooch food from the eagle. "Your bird friend seems to be able to get to your world. Why can't he take a note?"

Scott chuckled. "Knowing the bird, I can assure you, we will have to bribe him with something shiny."

Dr. Moore fished through his bag. He produced a small opal ring. "I bought it for my young daughter, but she died of consumption. I have carried it a long time."

Scott took it with reluctance. "Maybe we can get it back from the bird later, sir." He wrote on a piece of his shirt. *I have a severe infection. I need some penicillin or I could die. Send some with Shadow and send as much as you can.* He tied the note tightly to the ring.

The bird looked over the prize with an open beak. The raven loved the ring, but not the note. He tried to pick it off. He cawed when he couldn't remove it. He finally gave up and flew off with the ring.

Dr. Moore laughed. "Our fate lies with the bird. They will kill me if the girl dies."

The bird landed on the backyard patio table. Carol and her mother updated the police. A butterfly net captured the raven. The leader of the hypnotist students tried to take the ring from the bird but got pecked hard.

Before he could yell, the sergeant had shoved a gun in his back. "You are all under arrest. One of the men *you* shot has died."

The five students sat in a cell. One officer sat at a table. He faced them. They ate supper. The leader looked at his shiny coffee cup. He noticed he could reflect the ceiling light anywhere with it. It was the weekend. The police station had limited personnel.

There was an officer at the desk in front of the cell. The man was reading an E-book. He yawned. Two people in the cell were practicing their hypnosis inductions. The leader flicked light in the officer's face. One of the women put the other asleep with her dull monotonic countdown.

The officer's head bounced on the laptop. The hypnotists chuckled. An hour later they were in the officer's car. The officer was found naked in the DA's front yard the next morning.

The Raven and his ring were given to Mr. Thorburn. Mr. Thorburn's bridge partner was a doctor. He called in a prescription for him. His wife drove downtown to pick it up. The druggist was curious. He laughed, "That is a triple prescription. What… is your horse sick?"

She laughed. "Oh, not at all, We captured Bigfoot, and he has a nasty gash from jumping through our picture window. Apparently, he is a Metallica fan." She chuckled as she walked by the bewildered druggist.

She returned in time to see the raven walk past a row of colored earrings. He stopped in front of the pink ones and eyed them with obvious lust. Carol covered them with her hand and pulled them aside.

The pills were placed in a little bag with a note, *one every four hours for three days.* The pink earrings were put on top. The raven strained his neck to see what she was doing. A little handle made of a strong fishing line was secured to the top. The lazy bird didn't even try to pick it open. He knew who would open it for him.

The raven plopped on Scott's shoulder. He was asleep. The bird pulled his earlobe. The four girls giggled at him. He pretended to be asleep. Shadow became more aggressive. He yanked hard and squawked. Scott opened his eyes and rubbed his ear. "That hurt, you crazy bird."

Shadow picked up his package and dropped it in his lap. He opened it and was pleased to see the penicillin. He handed it to the doctor. He read the instructions and gave Scott and the girl each a pill. Scott gave the bird the pink earrings. He happily flew off.

Three days later, Scott and the girl were safe from infection. Now the problem was to get home. The leader was having some kind of ceremony for the magic pills that saved his young granddaughter's life.

The doctor told Scott to accept whatever they gave him. There was a period of dance and speech. Finally, Scott was brought forward. He was relieved when all they did was draw a small symbol on his forehead.

He walked back to Dr. Moore's sleep area. "They just painted some symbol on my forehead."

The Dr. smiled. "I am afraid not." He tossed a small rock at Scott. It should have hit him, but instead, it fell at his feet. "You have another problem He pointed to the girl. It is a tradition that the chief offers his granddaughter to you to be your wife." Scott looked shocked.

The doctor pointed at the four blue girls who smiled and giggled. "You also get her four maids. If you refuse, you will probably be on tomorrow's menu. Your only hope is to jump off the black cliff. The ancient people that lived here say it was a doorway through time."

Scott squeaked. "Did it really work?"

The doctor shrugged. "No one knows for sure. You can appear in any time period and anywhere. The blue beings say there are no skeletons at the bottom, but there is a permanent blue fog and they can't see beyond their outstretched hands."

Scott smiled. "So, the beings must use it, or why else would they check the bottom?"

Dr. Moore blushed. "Well, meat is scarce in the spring, and most of them hate berries."

Scott was shocked. "So, you are saying they eat dead people?"

The doctor chuckled. "We eat dead chicken and deer."

Scott looked at the four girls and shuddered. "So where is the cliff?"

He pointed towards the river. "We follow it to the first sharp turn. You will shiver when you see it." They walked a half mile and followed the sharp turn. The imposing black cliff caused Scott to gasp. He could see the motionless blue fog below.

They could hear noises behind them. The doctor sighed. "They will kill me. I led you here. We have to jump." He shoved a bag in Scott's pocket. He grabbed Scott's hand and ran to the edge. They glanced back once and jumped. Scott lost his grip on the doctor. He waited for the impact that would kill him.

Carol cried at Scott's eulogy. It had been a year since Scott disappeared. The ceremony was held in the backyard, just before sundown. Carol noticed most of the attendees were girls. She smiled. Scott would *like* that. The sergeant was there with his distraught daughter.

Scott woke up and felt for broken bones. He stood up and scanned the area. He recognized it, but the tree line by the road was gone. He walked up the hill and saw the old portion of the cemetery. He remembered there were seven old graves on the top row. Now there were eight.

He walked down the row checking names. The eighth had his name. The date of his death was blank. He thought he might be dead. He didn't have any idea what death was like. He wanted to find his family. He walked down the hill to the road. A car went by. He could swear it had no wheels.

He felt a bag of something substantial in his pocket. It contained twenty gold coins. He whispered to himself. "Thank you, doctor." He walked down the road and stopped in his tracks. His house was gone. There was just a small park.

He walked down to it. There was a plaque. *In memory of the Thorburn family, murdered on October eighth, twenty fourteen.* He frowned. "That's not possible, that year has not occurred." He wiped tears from his eyes. He would have to be careful and not draw attention to himself. He might be considered the last link to the gold.

He saw a coin shop on Main Street. He didn't remember one being there. He took a coin out of the bag and strolled in. There was an attractive middle-aged woman there. "Can I help you?"

Scott nodded. "I have a coin to sell. My grandfather willed it to me."

She was shocked to see it was gold. "Wow, 1871 liberty head twenty-dollar gold piece, mint condition. Was he a collector?"

Scott shook his head. "He was a retired history professor, like the Indiana Jones character. He explored the Midwest."

She chuckled. "That explains why the coin is not graded and in a protective plastic holder." She looked it up on her phone. She noticed several coins of that year had appeared in town a hundred years earlier. She smiled at Scott. "I can give you eight thousand for it."

Scott chuckled. "I figured two or three thousand max."

She laughed. "Yes, maybe a hundred years ago. My name is Sandy Smith.

She held her hand out. Scott blushed. "Scott Thorburn."

Sandy asked, "Are you related to the people on the plaque?"

Scott smiled. "Distantly."

Though she was in her thirties, she was still a knockout. She gave Scott her business card and eight thousand dollars. He got seven thousand-dollar bills and a thousand in hundreds. He buried the rest of the coins under his grave. He chuckled. "This must be a first."

He tried to buy a newspaper but was laughed at. He went to a store and bought a phone and service. He was shocked when he saw the year was 2112. He went to the library and was pleased to see they still used laptops.

He researched the murders. They occurred several months after his incident. He figured it might have to do with the gold coins. He tried to figure out if Sadie died in the nineteenth century and if so, how she ended up in the coffin alive, in the twentieth century.

Sandy was also curious about the coins that showed up a hundred years ago. The coins were all from 1871 and in mint condition. She looked shocked. Four were found in the boots of a girl who was buried alive and dug up alive, who then vanished from the hospital.

Several other 1871 coins were given to Carol Thorburn by a raven for several pairs of her earrings. There was a picture of the Thorburn family. She chuckled. Scott looked like Scott's twin brother.

Scott got a room at the hotel. He paid cash and had no baggage or identification. The owner called the police to check him out. They found he had spent a lot of time on the library laptop. They took a photo and showed it around. They got a hit at the coin shop. Sandy told them he had sold a coin to her. She did her due diligence and found there were no coin robberies in the area for five years.

They decided to pull him in for a talk. An officer tapped a pencil and stared. Scott looked down to make sure his fly was up. There was a lot of laughter. The officer blushed. "Oh, that was funny."

A lieutenant chuckled and motioned him to an interview room. 'I am Lieutenant Long, and you are?"

Scott shook hands. "I'm Scott, I think. You're *not* going to believe my story, sir. If you have a lie detector? Hook me up. It will save time."

Long laughed. "We haven't used one of those for eighty years. Hell, I've never even *seen* one. We use a VSA system here." He saw Scott's expression and chuckled. "That would be Voice Stress Analysis. You never heard of it?"

Scott nodded. "I heard of it, but I thought it was only in the experimental stage."

Long put a device on the desk. "This is one. It has three lights. Green is for a true statement. A red light indicates a lie and a yellow light for undetermined."

He turned it on, along with a camera. "So why are you in our lovely little town?"

Scott sighed. "I jumped off a cliff into a blue fog and found myself back here."

Long was shocked to see the green light stay lit throughout the statement. He recovered. "What do you mean by, back here?"

"I was born here and lived where the park is currently."

"No house has been there for a hundred years, Scott." He saw a slight smile form on Scott's face. "What is your last name?"

"My last name is Thorburn. I was born in 2002."

The lieutenant noticed the light stayed green. "I'm afraid that is not possible, Scott; unless of course you truly believe your absurd story." He placed the camera directly in front of Scott and put the sensor in the picture behind him. "Start your story from the beginning up to your seat in this chair, now."

Long left the room to call the department's psychiatrist. He left the audio feed open. He came back five minutes later and found ten officers. They hung on every word. Their eyes pleaded with him. He chuckled. "Don't worry, I will let him finish, ladies."

Long played the video an hour later. He had the shrink beside him. They listened in silence. Pete the psychiatrist shook his head and laughed. "I can tell you this; he believed every word of his story."

Long started an investigation, but most of the information would be over a hundred years old. First, he checked the early movements of the boy. The Lieutenant found a man selling fish by the river, who saw Scott walk out of the cemetery. "He seemed surprised to see the park. He read the dedication and walked towards town."

He was told Scott sold a coin to Sandy. He talked to her. "It was a twenty-dollar liberty head gold coin. It was 1871 in mint condition." He was shocked by the date. She showed him the picture of the family she downloaded. "Anybody appear familiar, Lieutenant?"

Sandy told her teenage daughter, Sally, about the boy with the gold coin. She blabbed to her friends about him and how much her mother had paid for the gold currency. She had girlfriends with some rough boyfriends, who planned to steal the eight thousand dollars, one way or another.

SCOTT MEETS REGINALD AND THE GODDESS SALLY

Lieutenant Long decided to move Scott into his home, for his protection. Too many people knew about the cash and heard rumors about gold. Scott sat down for supper. "Lieutenant, I can take care of myself. I told you how I got here. Now I want to find out what happened to my family, and maybe change the outcome."

His wife handed Scott some fried chicken. He took one bite. "Well, *maybe* I can stay a *little* while." The Longs had lost their only son in a car accident in 2102.

Mrs. Long asked, "What is that on your forehead, Scott?"

Scott blushed. "I got tattooed by some, ah, people."

The lieutenant snorted in his coffee. He examined it. "You know, I didn't notice that. It looks like Sumerian, to me."

She laughed. "My husband has a history degree. I have an art degree. My name is Lucy and my husband, off duty, is Lee."

After dinner, Scott decided to visit the park before sunset. He had placed the seven thousand dollars in Long's secret floor safe. Scott stared at where his house used to be. He could almost see his sister doing homework on the patio.

He was rudely interrupted by three teenage thugs. They tried to punch him, but their fists never reached him. To the thugs, it felt like hitting cement. Scott fell to the ground. He pretended to be hurt. Their car burst into flames. They heard a distant police siren and ran off.

The police arrived and cuffed Scott. An eighty-year-old woman with winged glasses named Donna ran outside to the sidewalk. "No, you idiots, not him. He was the one that got punched and um… hit with an aluminum bat. I could tell by the sound. Wait, you're not hurt, but I heard the hits."

Scott blushed. "They just grazed me with the blows, miss."

The flattered woman giggled but then realized what he was doing. She bristled. "Bullshit. They walloped you; you should be bleeding or dead."

The police laughed at her. "The UFO guys from last week's invasion must have protected him."

She double-fisted. "There really were giant blue men last week, and they looked for meat. I was lucky that I am svelte. They told me with their minds."

Scott returned to the Longs. He saw the scanner. "Just some kids. They tried to get some money. They ran off when I fought back."

The concern left both their faces. Lucy laughed. "Well, be careful out there. Some of these kids would sell your body parts for a latte."

The owner of the car sat opposite a sergeant. "I parked my car and went for a walk. I came back, and it was covered in flames. A boy approached my friends and me. The little prick tried to rob us."

The officer chuckled. "We have a witness, who begs to differ."

Reginald chuckled. "You don't mean the old bat next to the cemetery that called into the radio station claiming she had giant blue men try to eat her poodle?"

The officer chuckled. "The lad didn't press charges. He is being investigated as we speak. I just want to know if there was anything unusual about him, off the record, of course. We might even throw in a report to your insurance company, that said the fire was not set."

He chuckled. "I can tell you this, sergeant, that boy can take punishment. It was a damn embarrassment."

Scott returned to the library, to research the deaths of his family. They were tortured for several hours, before being shot in the back of their heads. Their dog, Winston was also killed. He tried to protect them. There were five suspects, but no evidence to tie them to it.

There was something else a couple of years after the family's death. Someone had paid for a stone in the cemetery for Scott. He read the name and smiled. It was Dr. Moore. He had made it. Scott chuckled. His tombstone was next to Dr. Moore's original eighteenth-century reburial gravestone. He was sad to see the doctor only lived for three years.

He did not realize he was watched by a young woman. Sally was the same woman, whose girlfriend told Reginald that he had money. Her mother Sandy told her what she paid for the gold coin from Scott. She felt guilty about that. Her mother said the people named in the park were his distant relatives.

The Longs and Scott ate shish kabobs in their backyard. Scott went inside for more lemonade. Lee had shown his wife the video. "Obviously none of that can be true. He must have believed it since the light stayed green. Too bad he seems so nice." Scott reappeared with the pitcher.

Lee had copied all the microfilmed files on the murder, he gave them to Scott. "I know you probably do not believe any of this." A large raven landed on the table and hopped over to Lucy. He eyed her earrings and pulled at one. She squealed. "Hey, that is my earring."

Scott realized he was not insane and grinned. "Are those earrings expensive?" A stunned Lucy shook her head no. "If it is my friend Shadow, he will trade for your earrings. His favorite color is red. Put them on the table in front of you. He is pretty honest... *if* it is my friend Shadow." He walked around them and suddenly flew off.

Ten minutes later he was back with a chunk of blue sea glass.

Scott told her to shake her head and say *no*. The bird grabbed his glass and flew off. He came back with an antique shoe buckle. Lucy wanted to trade but shook her head no again.

The third time the raven brought an 1871 twenty-dollar gold piece in mint condition. Lucy nodded and the delighted bird grabbed his prize and flew off. The Longs were dumbfounded. Lucy shuddered. "My God, it is all true."

Lee grinned. His wife snickered. "I am afraid my husband is a sci-fi junkie."

He smiled. "I am in an x-file episode. I hope it is a two-parter. By the way, Scott, several officers copied your family's murder case. And several reporters are sniffing around. Your pal, Reginald, told everyone you were an alien. So far, nobody believes him."

The bird was back. This time, Shadow eyed the broiled steak tips. Lucy put out a few pieces for him and some water. Scott laughed. "The little mooch will be a permanent supper guest. I'd invest in some more colored earrings."

Several days passed. The press found out about the girl buried alive. They found out about the connection between the Thorburns and the bird. They found out about the lost 60,000 in stolen gold. They concluded Scott was a con artist trying to cash in.

Sally noticed the giant black bird come and go from Long's home. It usually carried something shiny. She knew Scott stayed there. She spotted all of the electronic security cameras. Sally figured they brought them for his protection. She chuckled. "If you can handle Reginald and his goons, electronic protection is overkill."

Several police officers examined the Thorburn murders of 2014. They looked at it off duty, so the lieutenant didn't mind. "Keep me updated. Oh, find out where the reporters got their information."

Word got out that Scott had sold a nineteenth-century coin, which might have been from the robbery to Sandy Smith. A group of reporters jammed the entrance to her shop. She let them take pictures of the gold piece, to get rid of them.

Meanwhile, Reginald had informed the Russian mob that Scott knew where a fortune in stolen gold was hidden. He would get the five percent finder's fee if they secured the gold.

One of the mob's men was a computer hacker. He figured out the value of the gold now. "It was worth twenty dollars an ounce then, so that is three thousand ounces. Gold now is two thousand an ounce. The spot value is six million dollars. The coins are liberty heads in mint condition valued at twelve thousand a coin."

The man smiled, "That's thirty-six million dollars, boss, provided we didn't saturate the market."

The leader nodded. "This Scott boy was the only link to it. We must grab him alive. Reginald says he stayed with a police lieutenant. He gave me the address. He thinks the boy is a UFO alien. We will have to *abduct* him." He laughed.

Scott bought an ice cream soda and sat in deep thought in the downtown park. He was not sure what to do. A silhouette blocked the sun. "So how did you get away from Reggie? Nobody ever gets away from Reggie."

The figure moved to his left. Sally was blonde and about fifteen. She chuckled when he looked at her butt. "So, you're the famous Scott I have heard about?" She frowned and looked at his butt and nodded.

He laughed. "Yes, I deserved that. Yes, I am the hottie, Scottie."

She curtseyed. "And I am the love goddess, Sally. So why are you in town, Scott, besides the off chance to meet me, I mean?"

"To research my family's murder. I am here by accident, albeit a happy one."

"Hello? They died a *hundred years ago*. You don't look old enough to buy beer."

He handed her a family picture. She nodded. "I have seen this picture before. My mother downloaded a copy."

He was surprised. "Mom doesn't, as a rule, get young men selling twelve-thousand-dollar coins."

He chuckled. "She only gave me eight."

Sally laughed. "Anyone else would only have got five."

Scott frowned. "Why did she give me eight?"

Sally chuckled. "She thinks you are boyfriend material. So, what are you really after?"

Scott looked out at the red sun. "I want to find the killers and maybe stop the murders."

Sally snorted. "What do you mean by that? They were murdered a hundred years ago. You can't go back in time."

Scott smiled. "How do you explain me?'

Sally laughed. "So what? You happen to look like a relative."

Scott shook his head. "Look at the handsome devil's left hand. There is a two-inch scar from being spiked in a little league baseball game."

Sally snickered. "All I see is a wedding ring. Oh, you mean the young boy? I guess the scar is similar. He probably got stabbed by a disgruntled girlfriend. Well, I got to go and help my mom."

Scott ate a burger at supper and sighed. "This Sally thinks I am crazy."

Lucy laughed. "Well, that didn't take long."

Scott blushed. "She was curious why I was here,"

Lucy laughed. "Sure, she was."

Lee chucked. "We have no information on the killers. We have some fingerprints from a couple of pinky fingers and a few partial forefingers. I have several men who want to work on your case on their own time. They hope for a reward if you find the gold."

Scott smiled. "I'll pay them for the effort." Scott decided to walk down to the little park. Four men in a limo grabbed him. Two giant blue men caught them and headed up the hill.

Crazy Donna called the police. "And then two ten-foot giant blue men grabbed the four gangsters and ran up the hill. Don't laugh moron. Their car is here, and it's running smart ass."

Two policemen arrived and checked the car. It was stolen.

Scott played stupid. "It must have happened right before I got there."

Donna turned red. "Bullshit. They grabbed you." She pointed to the hill. "The blue men carried a guy under each arm. They ran fast. I guess they like their meat fresh."

The police sighed and took out flashlights. They found a giant print. One laughed. "Shit, Dave, this print would put Bigfoot to shame." They found three wallets on the hill. The footprints stopped abruptly on the other side.

Dave measured the stride. "The distance is twenty-four feet, Mike. The ground is soft on the hill so where did they go?"

Donna followed them up the hill. She snickered. "The big bad policemen never heard of a *mother ship?*" The two men looked at the sky and returned to the stolen car to lock it up.

The next afternoon Scott sat in the shade in the park. He read old files. He was surprised to be handed a milkshake. Sally smiled. "I am surprised to see you. I heard you were abducted."

Scott chuckled. "I heard four men got abducted, and I got *that* from the police."

She looked at the files next to him. "Can I peek?"

Scott chuckled. "Sure, I need all the help I can get."

A half-hour passed. "Is this all you got? You need more. You say you were chased. You saw nothing else?"

Scott frowned. "At the time I *was* being shot at. I saw two cars pull into the yard. One with people, I had seen. The second five people I didn't know. I saw them shoot at the first car. The police pulled in while I followed Shadow over the hill."

Sally frowned. "Who is Shadow, a clingy girlfriend?"

Scott chuckled. "I never had a girlfriend."

She laughed and smiled wickedly. Scott blushed. Sally frowned. "I think we need the full police report for that incident."

Scott did a double-take. "I can look it up on my computer. The lieutenant gave me a password." He looked up the event. "The police ran thumb scans at the time." He downloaded them. "Let's run them through AFIS."

Sally asked, "What is AFIS?"

Scott scoffed. "Your boyfriend is Reginald, and you don't know what AFIS is?"

She flinched. "Reggie is *not* my boyfriend. I used him to scare my mother. She is happy to let me date other boys."

Scott grinned. "You must have good taste in boyfriends."

Sally blushed. "That was *if* that situation ever came up. She *likes* you." Scott blushed. The computer beeped several times.

Three faces came up, and Scott's screen captured them. Sally frowned. "What good are they? The people were already dead. Are you going to shoot their descendants or something?"

Scott was in deep thought. He whispered to himself. "Maybe I can go back to the event."

Sally chuckled. "So, your name is not Scott Thorburn, but Dr. Who?"

Scott frowned. "Well, not me *personally*, but maybe a *friend*... if the price is right." He chuckled.

At supper, Scott told the Longs how Sally was interested in his parent's murder. The lieutenant was intrigued. "Why don't you invite her to a cookout tomorrow night at, say, six?" Scott frowned.

His wife laughed. "Wow, she is *that* beautiful?"

Scott sighed. "Well, if I run into her in the park, I'll ask, but I wouldn't bet on it."

Lucy enjoyed herself. "You will, and she will accept with false reluctance."

Lee laughed. "She is always right. It is a gift."

Sandy was happy, her daughter liked Scott. He might be eccentric, but he didn't have a rap sheet or a gun permit. She hoped she would stay interested.

Scott arrived in the park with a bag and laptop. Sally was already there. She looked different. She chuckled at his confusion. "I changed my hair."

She saw the bag. "Is that for me?"

Scott chuckled. "No, not exactly. I'm afraid it is for Dr. Who."

Sally couldn't stand it. "Can I look?"

Scott smiled. "You can if you come over to the Long's for a cookout at six."

She blushed. "I guess I can, but I have to clear it with my mom." She looked in the bag. It was full of colorful imitation earrings. "So, you're telling me Dr. Who likes costume jewelry?"

Scott chuckled. "Yes, I am, and maybe I can prove it to you." He looked through the bag. He took out a pair of ruby teardrop earrings. "Wear these to the cookout."

Sally smiled. "You mean just the earrings?"

Scott snickered. "I don't think the lieutenant's wife would like it, even though she is beautiful too." He realized what he had said and blushed.

She chuckled. "I have to help my mom clean at the store. I'll see you at six." She kissed his cheek and left. He felt his cheek turn red where she had kissed him

Scott couldn't think and went back to the Long's. Lucy saw him approach. "I gather she said yes?"

Scot was surprised. "How did you know?"

She giggled. "The peach lipstick is a dead giveaway."

Scott frowned. "She did that on purpose." Lucy saw the bag on his laptop. "It's earrings for our flying friend. Don't wear earrings tonight. I have to convince Sally I am not a nut job."

Sandy was pleased. "What will you wear?"

Sally stopped dusting. "Something that goes with red earrings, I'm afraid."

"But you have no red earrings. You hate red."

"Scott asked me to wear them."

"Kinky."

"No, I think he has a reason for it. He wants to prove he is not crazy."

"Look, I don't want to know kissy stuff, but I *have to know* why the red earrings."

"Okay, mom."

Sally knocked on the door. Lucy answered it. "You better get the smelling salts, Lee. Come in, Sally. The boys are out back. You might give Scott a heart attack."

She saw the red earrings and chuckled. Sally whispered, "Why did he want me to wear red earrings, Mrs. Long?"

Lucy laughed. "I think he wants you to make a good impression on *Dr. Who.*"

Sally laughed. "I'm already nervous. That didn't help."

Scott turned white when he saw her. Lee pushed a much-needed chair under Scott.

Scott stuttered. "Ah, we have steak tips and salmon. We await our other guest."

Sally looked around and only saw four chairs. "Your other guest eats standing up?"

Lee chuckled. "You're right, Scott, she is smart. I'm Lee, and this is my wife, Lucy and you know Scott."

Sally smiled wickedly. "He's a work in progress."

Lucy looked above Sally and smiled. "Okay, we can start."

Sally looked around. "Don't tell me. Your guest is invisible?"

Scott chuckled. "Not quite."

The raven landed on Scott's shoulder. He peered at Sally bending his neck to get a better look. Scott smiled. "Sally, meet Shadow, and Shadow, meet Sally." The bird squawked. "That means he is charmed."

The bird liked salmon a lot. He had his fill and looked around. He hopped over to Lucy. She had no earrings. She felt guilty and blushed. He hopped over to Sally. Scott chuckled. "Turn to the side so the little beggar can see the red earrings. Shine them in the light." He tipped his head and looked. He grabbed at one. Sally squealed. "Hey, that… that's my ear."

The bird looked guilty. The raven flew off. Sally chuckled. "So, that's it?

Lee chuckled. "Well, I doubt it. He will try to trade for them."

Sally thought a moment. "What will he trade, a gum wrapper or something? Should I accept it?"

Scott chuckled. "That is up to you."

Sally smiled. "I'll trade even though they are from a person I admire."

Ten minutes later, Lucy glanced up. "Your little friend is back." Sally already had the jewelry off. The bird landed on Scott's shoulder and jumped down on the table. He hopped over to her and pushed something shiny towards her. She pushed the red earrings towards him. He squawked, took his prizes, and flew away.

She picked up her prize. "Boy, it is heavy." Her jaw dropped. "This is a twenty-dollar liberty head gold piece in near-mint condition. I can't take this."

Scott laughed. "Sorry, he won't trade back. You have to keep it. I happen to know he has a lot more."

She looked at the coin. "Where does the bird get them?"

Lee chuckled. "Scott says in Arizona, and I believe him."

Sally shook her head. "That is impossible. That is over 1500 miles from here."

Lucy laughed. "Impossible? How about Scott? He is young for his age. His fingerprints were in the system. They were in a time capsule buried a hundred years ago." The night went quickly. At ten o'clock Scott decided to walk Sally home. They were accosted by Reginald.

Sally noticed he kept looking around. He grabbed Scott, but he couldn't move him an inch. He felt hot breath on the top of his head. A thick blue arm picked him up and threw him over his shoulder.

Crazy Donna ran out with a broom and hit the giant. "Hey, fatso, you're scared my dog, Fifi." He turned towards her and growled. She looked at him. "I have to say, I've seen bigger." She limped back to her house. She swore up a storm and slammed her door.

The 911 line lit. "Fifth precinct, what is your emergency?" He whispered to the sergeant, "It's crazy Donna." He put the call on speaker.

Donna yelled. "I heard that, moron. A blue alien just grabbed Reginald. Yes, I am sober. He scared Fifi. I chased him off with a broom. Huh? He is ten feet six inches tall with a small…"

"A small what, Donna?" His mouth dropped open. "You can't say that on a 911 call, ma'am."

Donna chuckled. "I have two witnesses; that liar Scott and some blonde hooker."

Scott looked down and saw Sally had fainted. He sighed with relief. Scott got her to her feet and helped her get home. He made sure she didn't drop her coin. She went through the door in a daze. Her mother was concerned.

Scott blushed. "Reggie tried to rob us. You'll never see him again. I think she was shocked by the encounter."

Sandy chuckled. "*My* daughter doesn't shock, Scott."

Scott smiled. "I am sure your right, ma'am."

Sandy snickered, "You have gallantry." Scott left.

She found her daughter in the kitchen. She had an empty glass in front of her. "If you want the *story*, I need a glass of wine, Mom."

Sandy stared at her. "It better be good, or you wash the cabinets."

Sally chuckled and tapped the glass.

Sandy grabbed a glass for herself. "Okay, let's hear it."

Ten minutes later, Sandy tossed her daughter a cloth and chuckled. "A bird traded a trinket for your earrings. So, he is a smart little bird. What did he give you, something shiny?"

Sally nodded. She dropped the coin in the cloth and pushed it back to her mother. She picked up the gold piece, and her jaw dropped.

Sally smiled, "And mom, that's not the best part." Sandy gave her another half glass. She took a full one.

'Scott didn't want me to walk home alone. We walked by the Thorburn park and Reginald tried to rob us. He grabbed Scott and couldn't move him an inch. He got mad and yanked hard. He still failed to move him."

Sally finished her wine. "Then a ten-foot-tall blue man with horns appeared out of nowhere and grabbed Reginald like a rag doll. He licked him with a long blue tongue. I swear he tasted his mom. Then Crazy Donna came out with a broom and hit the giant and swore he scared her dog, Fifi. The blue man ran over the hill with Reggie. I pretended I fainted. Scott wasn't afraid at all."

Sally smiled. "And I have a lot of witnesses." Her mom wiped the table with the cloth and tossed it in the hamper.

Sandy gave her a look. Sally stared out the window. "I know, mom. He told me he would soon disappear, and I would never see him again. He had to go back and try to save his family."

Sandy sighed and decided to eat her "mother" speech. Sally smiled at her and sighed.

Scott was quiet at supper outdoors. The raven showed up. He hopped on Scott's shoulder and pecked his ear. "I don't wear earrings, dude." The bird landed in front of him. The Longs watched, amused.

Scott sighed. "I need to know if you understood me." He got a gentle peck once. The bird tipped his head and stared into his eyes. He shrugged, "Show me yes." The bird pecked him once. "Show me no." The bird pecked him twice.

He smiled. "I need to go back to the day before my family got killed. Can you bring me back there?" He got one peck. "Can I leave tomorrow?" He got one peck. The Longs chuckled.

Scott drank some lemonade. "Okay, the big question, what will it cost me?" He dumped his bag of earrings in a white bowl. The bird looked in awe with an open beak. Scott smirked. "So how many pairs will it cost me?" The bird sauntered around the dish.

Lucy asked, "Do you think he understood you?"

Scott chuckled and shrugged. "I think we are about to find out. So, Shadow, how many? Are two enough? He got two taps. "Okay, Shadow, how about *five*?" He was surprised to get one tap.

Shadow carried two orange earrings and put the pair on a saucer. He then took two pairs of red, a pair of blue and green. He squawked once and flew off with the first pair. He secured a set every ten minutes. Lucy put an extra pair of pink in his dish. He finished bringing the green and saw the pink ones. He walked around the saucer and finally took the pink set.

Ten minutes later he brought back a gold coin. Lee was shocked. "A wild bird that can count, and has ethics freaks me out." The bird pecked him once on the hand and flew off.

Scott chuckled. "I guess I leave tomorrow." He left a small box with a bow for Sally. It was heavy. He was gone when the Longs got up. He left them the bag of earrings and a note, *I'll try to come back.*

The Lieutenant got to work late. A patrolman knocked on his door. "Sir, I tracked all the information Scott downloaded." He placed the paper on his desk. "There was the expected stuff, but he also downloaded your son's picture and accident information." He laughed. "Why would he do that lieutenant?"

Sally went over to the Longs. She found Scott had left. Lucy struggled to carry the package to her. Sally was shocked by the weight. There was a note. "*I'll come back if I can.*" The package contained eighteen coins. She struggled home. Her mother looked at the coins with lifted eyebrows. Sally laughed. "Scott didn't even *kiss me.*"

SHADOW TAKES SALLY FOR A RIDE

Sally sat in the park alone and stared at the river. The raven peered at her for half an hour. He floated down to her bench. She was shocked but happy to see him. He let her pet his head. She talked to him. "I miss Scott terribly." She had a tear run down her cheek.

Shadow tipped his head at her. He flew a few feet and looked back. She just looked at him. He flew back to her and pecked her hand. She yelped and rubbed it.

He squawked and flew a few feet away. Sally looked at him. He opened his beak and looked at the sky. A four-year-old little boy laughed. "He wanted you to follow him somewhere." He looked at his mom. "Boy, Daddy is right about blondes."

His mother laughed. "You're blond."

He smiled. "Daddy says it only applies to women. Boy, daddy is smart."

She smirked. "Mommy will have to congratulate Daddy on how smart he is tonight, dear." They left.

Sally chuckled. "Fine, Shadow, lead the way." The sunset approached. The bird led her to the edge of the cemetery. He landed in front of her. He walked five steps and vanished into thin air. She gasped. The bird reappeared after a few seconds. He just stared at her. She felt in her pocket for her lucky gold piece.

She started to hyperventilate. She looked down at the raven and sighed. "Sorry, mom." She took some steps. The raven had disappeared. Nothing seemed different. She laughed to herself. "The kid was right. I am an idiot."

She thought the breeze felt strange. She walked over the cemetery hill. She was shocked to see a house where the little park should be. A dog trotted up the hill to her. She patted him and looked at his dog tag Lancaster 2014. She broke out in a sweat.

A young girl trotted up the hill. She appeared to know her. "Sadie, where have you been? Are you all right?"

Sally mumbled. "I don't know you."

Carol chuckled. "Hello? It is me Carol from the hospital, sister of Scott."

Sally realized she had seen her picture. "My name is Sally. You are Scott's sister. People are on their way to torture and kill you in twenty-four hours. This will sound absurd. Scott came back a hundred years in time with the help of a bird to save your lives."

Carol chuckled. "It sounds like my pal, Shadow."

Sally was shocked. "Yes, Scott called him Shadow. The bird offered me the chance to follow, and I took it."

Carol smiled. "Why? What is he to you?" Sally blushed. Carol snickered. "Yes, my brother is a chick magnet."

Sally was alarmed. "He has a *lot* of girlfriends?"

Carol shook his head. "No, he's never had one. He likes smart girls, and I am the only one in town. Well… until now." Sally smiled.

She went into the house with Carol. She was introduced to the family. She told them everything that had occurred in their time. Scott had pictures of the three of them. The mother asked about Scott. They hadn't seen him. Sally was intrigued. They seemed so calm about the murders.

Carol chuckled. "My brother said he had some unusual friends. The laws of physics don't apply to them. I personally have never met any of them."

Sally chuckled. "What about Shadow?"

Carol laughed. "I stand corrected."

Sandy had called the police to inform them her daughter was gone. "She might have left with Scott Thorburn." She went over to the Longs home to see if Scott was there.

Lucy told her that Scott left the night before. Sandy cried. "Scott must have taken her."

Lucy shook her head. "No, Scott went into a dangerous situation. He would not risk her life. Maybe she followed him."

Sandy sighed. "Sally was capable of that."

Scott sat on a park bench facing the police station. He waited for two hours. Scott saw the sergeant walk out the door. He whistled at him. The officer looked shocked but walked over.

He shook his hand. "We thought you were dead, son. Where have you been?"

Scott chuckled. "I had some people shoot at me, sergeant. I was transported somewhere I couldn't return from. Thanks to the black raven. I made it back to stop people who want to kill my family." He saw the badge and chuckled. "I mean, Chief Smith. I want you to announce you found me. You can make up some weird story for the press."

The chief grinned. "I always wanted to do that." The smile scared Scott.

Scott sipped a coke. "They think my family knows where that gold stolen in the last century was hidden. They are wrong. They don't know, and the angry group will kill them within twenty-four hours. Here are some pictures and info on three of the five people. I am going home. When they know I'm alive, maybe they will come after *me*."

His family expected him. He was surprised. "How did you know I returned? Did Shadow tell you?"

Carol chuckled. "No, your girlfriend did."

Scott turned red. "My what?"

Sally stood behind him. She laughed. "Your sister seems to think I am your girlfriend."

Scott blushed. "How did you get here?"

Sally smiled. "Your little friend Shadow offered me a ride. I wanted to see how people lived a hundred years ago."

Scott sighed. "You shouldn't have come. It is dangerous for you."

Sally chuckled. "So, *you* are *not* in danger?"

Scott smirked. "You know the answer to that. Reggie and his boys couldn't even muss my hair."

Sally nodded. "Yes, but these people may have better weaponry than a switchblade and baseball bat."

The chief had a press conference. Scott, Sally, and his family watched it on TV. The officer came on with a bandage over his left eye and adjusted a microphone with a bandaged hand. Scott laughed. "Oh, brother..."

A hot female reporter raised her hand. "There is a rumor that Scott had been abducted by some female aliens with ray guns. What do you say to that?"

The chief grimaced as he readjusted his mike. "I don't know who started these rumors, but in this case..." An imposing seven-foot man in a black suit and sunglasses whispered in his ear. The chief whispered towards the mike. "You mean I can't talk about the giant nude woman who shot me with the ray gun?"

The chief sighed. "We found Scott tied to a tree in the woods below the cemetery. He had a sunburn and some gold coins he said he found. He is the only person alive who knows where the gold coins are hidden. He returned home to recover with a ten-foot-tall blue alien from the future."

The irate man in black covered the mike with his six-fingered hand. Two officers assisted the "wounded" chief off the podium. He apparently had a foot injury from the nasty alien confrontation. The unknown man in black whispered into the mike in a metallic voice, "This press conference is over."

Carol chuckled. "It *is* an election year. So, Scott, they tore your clothes off and tied you to a tree, and then what?"

Scott frowned. "Oh, that was funny, sis."

An hour later there was an all-terrain vehicle with tinted windows parked fifty yards down the road. Scott chuckled.

Sally shook her head. "What is wrong with you people? That car probably contains armed killers."

Mr. Thorburn called the police. "There is a suspicious car parked on our road with tinted windows. I think they are the people after Scott. Tell the chief they are likely armed."

Only one police car showed up. Carol murmured, "The idiots came alone." Both officers got out. One stood back behind the door with his gun unlatched. The man behind the door's partner laughed at his caution. A shot rang out, and the man behind the door fell from a foot shot and was finished off. His partner was shot from the driver's side window.

The house had a hidden nineteen-fifties-era air raid bunker in the cellar. All went in except Scott. He had his new dirt bike ready for action. He headed right towards the car and tossed a couple of coins at them. He gunned the cycle up the sandy hill.

Most of the people followed Scott, but two headed to the house to take hostages. They found no one there. They went outside to check on their friends. They were gone. They went back inside and caught the family as they exited the bunker.

A woman prepared to shoot Carol. "Sorry, no witnesses. Sally lunged at the woman and got killed in the effort. Mr. Thorburn grabbed the weapon and shot the surprised woman's partner before he could draw. The woman got her back up out of her ankle holster, but he blew her away.

They checked Sally. She was dead. They ran out to check on Scott, but everyone was gone. His bike had minor damage and was found on the back side of the hill.

They went back inside and were shocked to see Sally's body disappeared. The police arrived and picked up their officers and the two bad guys Mr. Thorburn shot. They hadn't bothered to call the chief about the call for help or about Scott, Sally, and the other bad guys' disappearances.

Sally opened her eyes and saw Shadow peering at her ears. She was shocked to see several giant blue women look at her. She gave a piece of jewelry to each woman. They giggled and left. One remained and glared at her. It was the leader's giant granddaughter.

An old man behind her laughed. "She knows you are Scott's woman."

Sally blushed. "So everyone keeps telling me."

Dr. Moore chuckled. "Then why do you have a drawing of Scott in your pocket. An excellent one I might add. That woman found it in your pocket. She was the leader's granddaughter."

Sally suddenly realized she must be dead. She felt her chest for a bullet wound. The blue girl gave her a derisive laugh.

"I am Dr. Moore. Your bird friend brought you here. You have been healed by me and the blue being's magic violet water. The blue beings saved your life, my dear."

Sally looked surprised. "Why would they save me?"

The doctor smiled. She chuckled. "Let me guess… because I was Scott's woman. My name is Sally." Dr. Moore laughed. "Scott did the leader a great favor. His daughter was by tribal law about to marry the evil witch doctor. Scott came along, and the woman called off her wedding.

The angry witch doctor tried to push him over the waterfall. Scott ducked, and he fell over. Their bodies were too dense to allow them to swim. The witch doctor drowned."

The doctor sipped some fermented berry juice. "Scott made it clear, he was not getting married. The leader made a show of chasing Scott and even tattooed him on the forehead. He will always protect Scott in both worlds." The daughter stared at her with some friends. Sally smiled and put the picture on a rock. The woman snatched it and left.

Shadow landed in front of her and squawked. The doctor nodded. "The bird said you must leave now. The daughter and her friends are here to kill you. You have to jump off the black cliff. Scott had to do it and survived."

They hurried to the imposing black cliff with the blue fog. Sally looked down. "You are crazy." The blue women closed fast. The raven yanked her ear, and she went over the side and screamed. A shadow flew gentle circles downward.

The bird stood on Sally's chest. He peered down at her. It was a cold moonlit evening. She woke. "Where am I? I'm freezing to death." The raven dragged an old blanket over near her. She smelled horse on it. She pulled it over her.

Sally woke from a troubled sleep and found the raven. He squawked and walked in front of her. She trudged behind him for a hundred yards and found a skeleton with a broken leg. It leaned against a dried tree stump. She grimaced. "That is so gross."

She started to leave, but the raven stopped her with a caw. He hopped forward and tapped the ground hitting metal. Sally kicked the sand and found a canteen, a quarter full of stale water. She took a long drink and filled her hand for the raven. He drank, cawed, and flew west.

She sighed and followed. The sun was hot enough to make the sand hot to touch. The bird flew back occasionally to check her progress. She struggled for three hours. She fought the urge to drink the water.

Sally heard a noise and found an old Indian staked to the ground. She made sure he was alone and pulled out with the help of a rock. Sally gave him the last of her water. He tried to give some back to her, but she motioned for him to drink it. The Indian emptied the canteen. He smiled at her and gave her a small necklace made of volcanic glass. He then trotted off into the hills.

Sally struggled for an hour with no water. She felt her canteen slowed her down. She must have a hallucination. But the canteen was heavy. She checked it. It was full of cold water. She whispered to herself, "But I gave the Indian all my water. I must have stumbled upon a spring." She took two large gulps and trudged after the raven.

Meanwhile, Scott hit the ground and sprinted. The killers were fifty yards behind him. They slowed down. A man looked around. "Where are we? Where did that little delinquent go?"

The woman smiled. "I'll tell you where we are, we are at the shiny rock and a lot closer to the gold." They started to follow Scott.

They were startled by the noise to their left. The three men went to check it out and found an Indian staked to the ground with rawhide straps. The Indian asked for water. They laughed and kicked sand on him. They went back to trail Scott. The Indian nodded and disappeared in a gust of blown sand.

Scott's four pursuers had company. A man laughed at the woman in short heels. "I'm glad you know where the oro is, chica. I would hate to give you to my men. They stink."

His men smelled each other and shrugged. They disarmed the three men. One of his men sniffed them and giggled. "Poncho, they all smell like women." The three men blushed.

The hypnotists looked over the bandits. They had no chance to get their guns back. The woman looked around like she was searching for landmarks. The leader chuckled. "You are a liar, chica."

The woman was a smartass. "You're used to your women's lies."

Poncho chuckled and shot her between the eyes. He smiled. "Are there any more funny gringos?" He got dead silence.

Scott followed the bandits. He was shocked to see Sally stumble into their camp. Poncho smiled. "We have another target and a pretty one, no? Do you know where the oro is, chica?" She shook her head.

One of the men noticed the full canteen. The water was ice cold. He tasted it. There was no sulfur taste. "Poncho, taste her water."

Poncho smiled. "Where did you get the water, chica? You must know this desert good. Well, you rest, while I take care of the little girly men."

He motioned with his head towards the strongest man. He knew he would have to kill him as a lesson to the other two. "Give the gringo a silver coin." He had him hold it out to the side. Poncho fired and missed by two feet. "Maybe I'm too close." He backed up ten feet and took a long drink of tequila. He missed by three feet.

He shook his head. "Maybe the coin she too big." His man gave the man a tiny coin. He took another giant swig of tequila. His men helped him back up ten more feet.

The man shook his head. "He held the coin over his heart. "Here you go, Deadeye."

Poncho smiled with his dead eyes. He motioned to his man with a flat hand and turned it ninety degrees. The bandit had a big smile. He flipped the coin sideways and extended the man's arm straight out two feet in front of his chest. Poncho became serious. "If you don't move you will live. If you do move, you will die, gringo."

Poncho had a fast draw, even when he was drunk on tequila. The coin split the bullet in half, and both pieces missed him. The man jumped up and down. Poncho shot him in the air between the eyes. He shook his head. "I guess my English is not so good."

The other two men pleaded for their lives. "All we know is you go north beyond the large, black glass rock."

Poncho smiled. "You sleep on your answer, gringos, and make peace with God."

The next morning after some bacon and beans the two men were staked to the ground. A hundred-pound slab of sandstone was placed on each man's chest. Poncho smiled. "We believe you, so we give you a chance to live. A small one, but a chance."

The young man smiled. "They let us live, Mike. I can't believe it."

Mike snorted. "Look where you are, Einstein."

His friend persisted. "So, you say we will die of sunstroke?"

Mike laughed so hard he couldn't breathe. "No, moron we get to drown in the desert. We are in an arroyo, and the noises are cumulonimbus clouds."

The men were surprised to see the old Indian stumble in. He chuckled and gave them water. They thanked him. He pulled over a rock to sit on. Mike smiled. "You speak English, Indian?" He just got a blank stare. He laughed. "The stupid Indian will die here with us."

The young man was horrified. He could hear the thunder get closer. "We kicked sand in his face, and he still gave us water. We can't let him die. Sir, you have to leave now."

Mike gave his friend a derisive laugh. A loud roar of water approached. "The surf's up Einstein." The Indian stared at him unconcerned. The wall of water hit.

Mike was blasted out from under the sandstone and crushed against a rock by a giant tree root. The young man noticed him and the Indian were not even hit. The sandstone slid off, and he stood up. The Indian disappeared.

Sally ambled along with the bandits. Poncho took a good look at the girl. "What strange clothes you have, chica. Where do you come from?"

"I come from Massachusetts, sir." One of his men searched her. He found a gold coin in her shoe.

He became excited. "Poncho, she has a gold coin, and it is the right year." He ran over and gave it to Poncho.

He tested it with his teeth. "Where did you get the coin?"

Sally blushed. "My friend and his black raven gave it to me."

Poncho smiled. "Was it a big bird?"

Sally smiled. "Yes, it was."

Poncho smiled. "I shoot him." He laughed with his men. Sally cried. Poncho saw the tattoo on her forehead. "Are you from an Indian tribe?"

She shook her head no. "I was captured by giant blue men, sir. They tattooed me."

Poncho laughed. "There are no blue giants, chica, but there is oro. You must know where it is." He played with his gun. "The only one who knew where the gold was is dead because you shot him. The bird knew."

Poncho started raising his gun. The old Indian stumbled in. He had a belt with one of the 1871 gold coins in it. The Indian seemed surprised to see them.

Poncho saw the coin. "You must know, where is the oro?"

Sally sighed. "I ran into him yesterday. He doesn't speak."

Poncho took out his pistol and aimed it at him. Sally stepped in front of the shocked Indian.

Meanwhile, the body of the raven was lying face up in the blistering sun. A hungry mountain lion approached and sniffed. It lost interest and wandered off. A large white owl floated down and inspected the dead bird. A soft blue flash hit the raven, and he popped to his feet.

Poncho looked at the Indian, who stared at Sally in front of him. "You understand me Indian?" He nodded. "Do you know where Black Rock is?" He nodded again and pointed to the northwest. "How far away is it?" The Indian pointed at the sun and moved his arm down. "It looks like three hours. I will give you four to find it, or you both die." The Indian smirked.

Scott followed the group. He hoped to find a dropped gun. Two hours later they arrived at Black Rock, a volcanic glass outcrop. Poncho smiled and took out his pistol. The Indian smiled and pushed Sally behind him. Poncho laughed. "The old Indian doesn't seem afraid to die."

He aimed. Sally jumped in front of the surprised Indian. He had no time to think and violently shoved the girl out of the way. With his concentration broken, he had no protection, and he was killed.

Poncho and his men laughed. They noticed the girl had vanished. Poncho swallowed hard and blessed himself. "She must be a *la Bruja*."

THE BRADY BUNCH TO THE RESCUE

The Indian woke up and chuckled at the owl and raven that were perched on his feet. He rubbed his chest and felt no wound.

"How could he miss from ten feet?" The owl gave him two hoots. He smirked. "Okay, he didn't miss, and you two saved me?" He got one hoot. "Is the young girl safe?" He got one hoot from the owl.

Meanwhile Snowflake, the magic owl of Victoria Brady, the adopted daughter of the Lancaster police detective, brought her new raven friend home. They sat in the old oak tree and stared down at an unconscious Victoria. Snowflake bent down and saw Victoria's new red zircon earrings. She chattered to the interested raven.

Shadow floated down to the porch rail and examined her new jewelry. He inched over and grabbed one. A shocked Victoria yelped. "Let go of my earring, you little crook." She brushed the bird back, and he fell to the ground.

She felt guilty and offered the bird a sugar cookie, but he refused to take it. He was eyeing her earrings again with obvious lust. Victoria chuckled and took them off. She offered them to the bird. He gently took his prize and flew off. She watched him disappear and returned to her book, but fell asleep.

Thunder and icy rain woke her up. She grabbed her book and ran into the house. Now that she was wide awake, she decided to read a while longer. She opened the book and was shocked to find a gold coin in it. It was an 1871 Liberty Head twenty-dollar gold piece. Snowflake hopped down to examine it.

Victoria looked at her. "Did you put the coin in my book?" She got two hoots. "Did the raven put it there?" She got one hoot and Snowflake looked back and flew out the window.

Meanwhile, Sally found herself in the center strip of a busy highway. A State Policeman saw her appear out of thin air. He wiped his sunglasses on his starched uniform. Yup, she was still there. He saw she was disoriented and hurried out to get her out of harm's way. She was in shock and sent to UMass Medical Center.

Sadie was put in hospital blues. She was given a strong sedative. Her eyes fluttered and closed. Her clothes were sent to the lab. They found an 1871 twenty-dollar gold piece in her shoe.

The lab gave them the report to the police the next morning. "The clothes are of an unknown fiber and style, but the socks and shoes were crudely made in an eighteenth-century style. There were traces of mesquite, sagebrush, and some horsehairs on her."

The head of the State Police looked at the lab results and grunted. He shook his head and sighed. "Get me Captain Brown on the phone, please." The delighted secretary made the call and held out her hand. A crisp ten-dollar bill was dropped on it.

Captain Brown's phone rang. Ten minutes later, the happy captain came out of his office. Detective Grogan's face turned white. "Oh no, the captain smiled."

Brady chuckled. "I wonder what they bribed him with this time."

Grogan saw the Augusta National golf cap on his gray head. "Oh God, he got another spooky case from the state police. It must be a hell of a bad one for them to give him rounds at Augusta National." Matt and Brady chuckled.

The captain frowned. "Gentlemen, the State Police asked us to take an amnesia case for them, since they are all backed up with ah… pothole duty."

Brady laughed. "That is the best they could come up with?"

The captain chuckled. "I will be taking a week's vacation to ah, visit my son in Georgia. Maybe I ah will play a little golf while I'm down there. Lieutenant Harvard will be in charge, and if anything happens to him, Brady's in charge. That is all."

Harvard came out of his office and smiled. "They will send the case over in the morning." Grogan fainted in his chair. Brady got home at six. Mrs. B. made him baked stuffed chicken for supper. His favorite. He chuckled to himself. *She knew about the case.* Victoria was out with her MIT friends.

Mrs. B. told him about the raven and Victoria's new earrings. The part about the bird and the twenty-dollar gold piece seemed a bit farfetched. He chuckled. "The stupid bird found a shiny object and made a trade, that's all. This town is three hundred years old. I'm sure a town that had four taverns, lost a lot of gold coins, dear."

Mrs. B. chuckled. "Victoria thinks the bird discovered a treasure, and she bought more earrings to prove her hypothesis."

The next morning Brady read the police report. A disoriented young woman was found wandering on the center strip of Route 2. The police took her to UMass Medical Center in Worcester. Her clothes were made from an unknown fabric and design. Brady chuckled when he read about the gold coin in her shoe.

Matt read over Brady's shoulder. "What is so funny?"

"A raven stole a pair of earrings from Victoria yesterday. It flew back later and dropped a gold coin in her book."

Brady called the State Police. The desk cop snorted. "We do not care about a stupid coin, Brady. We care about where the girl came from." Brady persisted. "Fine, Brady. It is an 1871 twenty-dollar gold piece."

Brady called his wife. "It is a Liberty Head twenty-dollar gold piece, honey. What? Oh, it's 1871."

Matt could see it on his face. "It is 1871, right?" Brady nodded. Matt chuckled and grinned. Grogan decided to put in for two weeks' vacation.

Brady and Matt headed to UMass Medical Center. The same smart-ass kid ran up to Brady's BMW. Brady grimaced. "I'm sorry, sir, you can't park here."

Brady saw his shiner. "What happened to your eye?" The young man frowned.

A voice behind Matt laughed. "The trustee's eighty-year-old mother, for some reason, didn't like the *old bag* moniker. She popped him good, and now he is on probation, hence the politeness."

Brady tossed him the keys. He watched the boy drive his car around the corner. He sighed, and they headed up to the young woman's room.

The two men were surprised to see her restrained and told she was just sedated. Her eyes were not calm and darted from object to object in the room. They finally settled on the two men.

The doctor entered and saw the terror in her eyes. He chuckled. "We had to medicate her. She snapped the restraints. She also broke her nurse's arm when she tried to escape."

The two men nodded unimpressed. The doctor snickered. "Her nurse is named Dwayne." He called out the door. "Dwayne, could you come in here for a moment?"

A deep voice asked, "Is she medicated, Doctor Snider?"

The doctor smiled. "Yes, she is, and there are two big detectives in here with me." A six-foot-eight giant entered the room and jumped behind the detectives. "Tell the officers how she broke your arm in three places."

She was restrained in bed, and the doctor wanted to give her a sedative. She panicked. I held her down. He gave her the shot, and she yanked her arms through the restraints and tossed me against the ceiling. I hit the railing on the way down, and my arm broke in three places. I looked up and she was asleep."

The doctor smiled. "The restraint is a thousand-pound test." Matt and Brady together couldn't break it. The girl gave Dwayne an icy stare. He saw it and left to continue his rounds. The doctor left. "You gentlemen have ten minutes before the sedative fully kicks in." He chuckled on his way out.

Matt laughed. "The good doctor thinks this will end badly." The young woman stared at them.

Brady turned on his recorder pen. He smiled. "Get a load of those green eyes."

"I get *ferfle ugly* when people grab me. That man was a *crooked stick*. He won't touch me again." She nodded and chuckled.

Matt looked up the strange words. "The first is *pissed* and the second, a *dishonest ruffian*. They are from the colonial era."

She looked Brady over. "What is wrong with my eyes, sir?" She twisted her hair in her fingers.

Matt looked at Brady and chuckled. Brady smiled. "We have not seen eyes so green. They are beautiful." She giggled.

She looked around. "Are thee witches?"

Matt chuckled. "Why do you think we are witches?"

She blushed. "This is all magic to me."

"You have not seen all this before?"

"Indeed not, sir. It is the work of the devil."

Matt shook his head. "No, it is not. It is just how our people live. What is your name?"

"Sadie Long sir."

"That is a pretty name. I am Matt, and my friend is Brady. So, where did you come from, Sadie?"

"I was in a sandy hot place, being questioned by men with large funny hats about *oro*? They also were questioning an old Indian. They tried to shoot him. I jumped in front, but he pushed me out of the way of the ball. I hope they did not kill him."

Brady frowned, "Do you know what year this is, Sadie?"

She thought for a minute. "It is 1750 or 1871, sir."

Matt chuckled at Brady. "Can you explain *that* to us?"

They looked at her. She was asleep.

Brady sighed. "No sleep for me tonight," Matt smirked.

Meanwhile, Victoria researched her coin. It was a fairly common coin. She persisted and, on the eighth Google page, she found a robbery. "Huh, let's check it out." There was a bank robbery, where sixty thousand dollars in newly minted coins were stolen from a Wells Fargo bank in Arizona, and all the coins were dated 1871. The thieves were never caught, and the money never recovered."

She checked archived Lancaster Police records, for laughs. She was surprised to get a hit from fifty years ago. It involved a young girl named Sadie. She was dug out of a three-hundred-year-old grave. "I wonder how they knew she was buried there?"

The case was vague. There was a reluctance to report it at all.

There was a name on the grave that was dug up, Doctor Moore. She rode her bike to the cemetery and found his grave on the highest hill of the site. It was in among the bell ringer's graves. "Well, that explains how they *might* have found her." She noticed a newer stone at the end of the row... and it had a bell too.

She wrote the name down, Scott Thorburn born in 2002, died, was blank. She checked the grave records. It was paid for by Dr. Moore. "That is strange... that stone was modern, and he requested a bell." The papers were a disappointment. The Sadie case intermingled with a Scott Thorburn missing person case. Neither was resolved.

She returned home and ate pizza when Brady sauntered in. He started to tell his wife about the unknown girl found on the highway. Victoria chuckled. "Hey, Pops, does her name happen to be Sadie?"

Brady was shocked. "How do you know? Did Snowflake tell you?"

She laughed. "No, just good old American ingenuity, I'm afraid. Maybe it is a different Sadie, but I doubt it. The State Police bribed Captain Brown with Augusta National for a reason… an excellent reason. We will compare stories after you hear it from her lips, that's after she asks you if you're married." She laughed. Brady blushed and felt the hair on his neck stand up.

The next day it was hot. Victoria checked the bell strings, and they were all intact. She suddenly realized she was lifting dead boney hands. Yuck, that is gross on so many levels. Thunder rumbled towards her followed by icy rain. She ran for the dilapidated cemetery hut.

She was surprised to hear the bells ring. Most were caused by wind. One rang a repeated pattern. She grabbed her umbrella and checked the graves. The doctor's ring was the repeater. She grabbed the leather cord and felt strong pulls.

That was enough for Victoria, she peddled her bike home. She took a hot shower. The storm passed. She sat on the porch with cocoa and waited for Matt and Brady to come home for burgers.

Matt and Brady were surprised to see Sadie fully dressed and sitting in a chair with no restraints. Sadie chuckled. "The head of the State Police told the doctor that you hotshot Lancaster detectives didn't need me restrained. He doesn't like you, constables." She laughed. They were surprised she picked up modern English so quickly.

Brady sent the audio from their first encounter to a linguist at Princeton. He said she used language from the colonial period, the late seventeenth to early eighteenth centuries. He laughed. "But we know time travel is not possible." Brady and Matt laughed. That raised eyebrows from the language professor.

Brady turned on his pen. The two detectives listened to her story. They hung on her every word. "Some of the story was told to me by Doctor Moore, my great, great, great, great grandfather. Parts of it were told to him by the blue giants."

Brady was confused. "What blue giants? And this grandfather would be dead long before you were born."

Brady looked at Matt. Brady smiled at Sadie. "We are all ears." She looked up at their ears with a confused stare. Brady smiled, "In our time, that means we would love to hear your story."

She looked at Matt. "What is Matt doing?"

Matt blushed. "I am checking old records to see if I can verify parts of your story as we listen. For example, what was the name of the tavern you worked in?"

"The Plantation House."

Matt shook his head. "Could it be, *Gull House*?"

She nodded. "*Aye*, in the olden days, they called it that."

Matt nodded. "It was built in 1680 and burned to the ground by the British around 1779." Matt saw her expression. "We won't ask any questions until you are done." He got a grim smile.

Sadie paused and sniffed. She continued her story and shuddered when she described how Roger and Robert buried her alive. She finished her tale. The two detectives stared at her.

Brady sighed. "That is quite a story."

She looked at the floor. "Your State Police didn't believe me either."

Matt cackled. "Oh, they believed you. That is why they gave your case to us. We believe you too, sweetheart."

She started to cry. Matt handed her a tissue and a box of solid white chocolates. "We thought you might like these. It is a candy." She smelled one. "Do I eat them?"

After a nod from Brady, she tasted one and grinned. "These are good."

Brady and Matt headed back to the house. "What do you think of her, Matt?"

Matt chuckled. "You mean apart from the crazy story? I like her a lot. There is something familiar about her."

Brady frowned. "I know what you mean."

They were surprised to see Victoria perched on the porch. An imposing raven sat on the rail peering down at them. Brady peered back. "Me friend." The bird relaxed, and Brady chuckled.

Matt looked around. "Where is your pal, Snowflake?"

She frowned. "My dear grandfather's usual bridge partner caught some type of alien sex disease. He needed a quick replacement. He bribed Snowflake to play with him. I don't know what she got, but she was psyched."

Victoria started to walk around to the back of the house. The raven hopped on her shoulder. She chuckled to the men. "It is not what you think. He plays *Get the Stick* with Larry, and shares his burgers with him." Larry wagged his tail and barked at his new buddy.

Victoria told them about the incident in the cemetery. They couldn't figure out how she knew about the graveyard since they were just told by Sadie. Brady chuckled, "Snowflake told you before she left?"

She laughed and scolded them. "You boys didn't use due diligence. You did not search old police records for similar cases."

Brady snorted. "Of course, we did. We went back for twenty-five years. The girl is only fifteen; do the math."

Victoria smiled. "But this case involved a fluid, time, boys." She handed them a report with their burgers. Larry's head was in Brady's lap immediately, and the raven was on Matt's shoulder, peering at his burgers. Victoria laughed. "They know easy marks when they see them."

Brady scoffed. "This report is fifty years old."

Matt chuckled. "Yes, it is, but look at the similarities. The name on the gravestone is a match."

Brady sighed. "I wish Snowflake was here." Larry nudged Brady with his nose. He gave him half a burger. Matt gave the bird a quarter and got scolded. He chuckled and threw in another quarter.

The nurse at UMass Medical had recorded the interview of the detectives. She figured Big Al would be interested in two hundred pounds of missing gold coins from the nineteenth century. She gave him the only copy of the interview, a major career failure. She didn't report for work the next day. She was found in the river, with a 38-caliber hole.

Brady and Matt figured the nurse had recorded their session and told someone. They decided to move Sadie to Brady's home for protection. Matt would stay there for the duration. Victoria was psyched. She never had a sister figure. They were about the same age and even looked alike.

On the ride back the two detectives realized they were followed. They turned onto Brady's dead-end road. Matt told Sadie to duck down. Brady hit the brakes, and they jumped out. They peppered the windshield with bullets which penetrated the car. The car backed out right through the stop sign and into the passing State Police Commissioner's Lexus.

Brady and Matt thought that was hilarious. Sadie popped her head up. "Does that sort of thing happen often?" The two detectives shrugged. Sadie snorted.

Brady was worried about Snowflake's absence. He made a few rules. "Tell your mother when you go out and take Larry with you and stay together."

The girls decided to visit the cemetery. Sadie had to learn to ride a bike first. That took a half hour. Sadie borrowed Brady's bike. They parked them halfway up the cemetery hill. Victoria let Sadie lead the way. She walked straight to the grave. "*Tis* where I was buried. You can see the repair of the stone Roger made when he tried to shoot Shadow, the raven."

Victoria laughed. "That is the name I made up for him."

Sadie chuckled. "There were four people in the coffin. The widow Wendy Whitlock, Doctor Moore's bones and clothes, Robert, the one who hit me with the rock, and the lovely Sadie." They both laughed.

Meanwhile, Scott woke up. He was tied to a dead tree and couldn't move.

Poncho smiled. "Give him some water."

His man looked at his clothes. "Look Poncho, he is dressed. like the dead girl."

Poncho's face brightened. "You must know where the oro is, yes?"

Scott's face dropped. "You killed Sally?"

Poncho laughed. "She wouldn't tell us what we wanted to know. We killed the old Apache too."

Scott took a deep breath. "What Apache? I don't know where the gold is. What kind of an animal shoots a young girl?'

Poncho sighed, "The same kind that shoots a young boy." He shot him. Poncho laughed. "I will run out of bullets." The bandits went back to search the canyons.

The old Apache found Scott's body and chuckled. He buried him under the old petroglyphed rock and left. Scott soon found himself sliding down a tunnel. "Oh no, not *again*." He splashed down into the violet water.

Meanwhile, the two girls noticed a black car parked at the entrance to the cemetery. Larry let out a low growl. Shadow peered down at them from Sadie's shoulder. Two large men got out of the car and looked around. Satisfied they were alone they headed up the hill with guns drawn. A rifle round hit a foot in front of them. The two men and the car vanished. Mrs. B. trotted down the path.

Sadie was in awe. She felt the rifle. "The musket is truly witchcraft. Where did the two men and car go?"

Victoria chuckled. Mrs. B. snorted. "I was to ask *you* that."

Mrs. B. chuckled too. "I didn't do anything. I just shot the ground in front of them to scare them away."

Victoria saw the raven in the tree. "Maybe Shadow did it."

Sadie looked surprised. "But he was only a bird."

Mrs. B. chuckled. "I know one bird that would beg to differ."

The two gangsters called Big Al. "We are in freaking Provincetown. They took our phones, wallets, and ah pants. We had to table dance to get money for this call, boss. What? I don't know, someone shot a rifle at us, and that is the last thing I remember. No, he didn't shoot me in the head… boss?"

The two girls told Brady and Matt what had happened. Matt told them the nurse was found dead on the pier. Harvard put a car on Sadie that contained two men who loved to shoot bad guys.

Sadie knew nothing of the fifty-year-old case. The girls rode with the police to the library. They looked through more old newspapers with different keywords. They found the rescued girl who said her name was Sally at first. She was uncontrollable and sedated for two days. When she woke up, she said her name was Sadie.

Victoria chuckled. "You do not remember any of this?"

Sadie shook her head. "So, I guess the dug-up person was someone named Sally?"

DIGGING UP SOME OLD FRIENDS

Victoria smiled. "Yes, I guess." Sadie stared at her, as they walked out to the police car. The deputies waved. The girls saw a Lincoln Continental pass, a man holding an AK-47 out the window. Victoria screamed at them as the Lincoln gained speed. Just as the gangster hit the trigger, the police car disappeared. The girls were hit. They glanced at each other and fell to the ground dead.

Brady had to tell his wife the girls were murdered. She wanted to see them. Matt sat on the porch with the Bradys and their shepherd, Larry. There was dead silence.

The Medical Examiner had them in cold storage and planned an autopsy. Matt and Brady were removed from the case by the assistant DA. They sat out in the backyard. They were shocked when Larry started to bark. He hopped around joyfully.

A curious Shadow came down to the railing. He listened to Larry with a tilted head. He suddenly hopped over to Mrs. B. and pecked her arm. She sobbed. "I'm not wearing earrings, Shadow."

They watched the bird hop down to Larry. He squawked at Larry, who listened intently. Larry walked over to Brady and yanked his arm. "I don't want to play, Larry."

He tried Matt, who tossed his favorite ball. He was surprised that Larry didn't chase it. Instead, he pulled on Matt's hand. "I never saw him ignore his ball before. He acted strangely for several days."

The bird hopped down and pulled Mrs. B. by the finger. She ignored him, and he squawked. Larry joined in and barked. Matt stood up, and the noise stopped. He sat down, and they started in again.

Brady sighed and stood up. They got quiet. "Okay, guys, now what?" Larry walked and looked back at Brady, who just stood there. Brady relented, and they all followed along. It became apparent that they were headed to the old cemetery. The raven hitched a ride on Mrs. B. It took almost a half hour to get there.

It was a warm evening. Larry walked to Doctor Moore's grave. He looked at the raven who shook his head and barked an order to Larry. He started to dig. The bird turned to the two detectives. They shrugged and went to the maintenance shed for shovels.

Matt and Brady dug. Ten minutes later they were pried off the coffin lid. There was a skeleton in colonial-era clothes. Matt looked at the bird. "Okay, Shadow, now what do we do?" The bird and Larry jumped in the coffin and looked up at them.

Brady sighed, "I can feel jail time. I gather we are supposed to bury the girls in the coffin?" He got a bark and squawk. The dog and the bird got out of the hole.

Matt nodded. "Let's go."

Brady sighed. "You don't have to help."

Matt smiled. "You risked your life last year for my sister. I wondered how I could pay you back... problem resolved. Let's go get our girls. Hey, maybe we can be cellmates."

Mrs. B. walked the dog home. The lazy raven rode on her shoulder. Brady called Harvard. He put their favorite sergeant, Smithy, on the desk.

Harvard sighed. "What have we to lose? Go for it. I'll take the hit. If we believe Sadie, which I do, we must make the effort."

Brady and Matt removed the bodies and returned to the grave. They gently put the girls in the coffin. Brady kissed their foreheads and sealed the coffin. They returned to the house.

The next morning the autopsy doctor went crazy. Harvard stonewalled him. "We have to examine them for ballistic evidence. After a week you can have them. We feel bad about the delay, so we are giving you a free week's vacation on Martha's Vineyard."

That stopped the doctor in his tracks. He looked at the floor. "Do I have to take my wife?"

Harvard smiled. "Take anyone you wish. As far as the world knows, you are on an undercover case for us."

A big smile crossed the doctor's face, "Deal."

Two agonizing days went by. On the third day, Larry's head popped up. His ears tipped, and he stared in the direction of the cemetery. He jumped up and down. He ran towards a sound only he could hear, the raven trailed. It began to rain. Harvard and the sergeant got Matt's call and were on their way up.

Brady, Matt, and Harvard took turns on the dig. If anything happened to them, they told Harvard and the sergeant to fill in the grave. They got to the top of the coffin. There were two bags of gold coins. They threw the heavy bags out and pried the lid off.

The coffin was empty, and there was a large hole in the side. An excited Larry jumped in the coffin and slid through the hole. Brady lurched for his leg but missed. His momentum made him fall through the hole, and Mrs. B. and Matt jumped in.

Harvard and the sergeant waited an hour in the rain and then covered the coffin and filled in the grave. The two men who tried to abduct the girls were found dead near Big Al's favorite pier. Victoria and Sadie sat with Doctor Moore. They heard the water get loud. Sadie chuckled. "It seems we have visitors."

Larry slid out of the cave. He howled with his tail between his legs. He yelped when he hit the frigid water. He heard the girls laugh and paddled to shore. He was excited and jumped back and forth between the two girls. He tried to lick their skin off.

A group of blue giants laughed at them. A minute later three people slid out of the cave. The giants howled with laughter. Victoria yelled at them from the shore. "They are friendly."

Matt saw a woman eat a man's foot. He snorted. "Well, the girls seem to trust them."

Mrs. B.'s teeth chattered. "I won't die from hypothermia." She swam to shore. The three people and the dog hugged each other. The insulted raven sat in a tree and squawked. Matt held out his arm, and the bird floated down and joined the reunion.

Meanwhile, Lieutenant Harvard was surprised to find two of Big Al's men in his apartment. They took his gun. "Look, Larry, he has a freaking nine mil, no wonder you guys always lost shootouts."

Big Al walked into the room. "So, why did you skip the funeral?"

Harvard said, "It was the wish of the family to have no fanfare."

Al smiled. "That seems logical enough. Now let's hear you explain why you dug up the grave?"

Harvard chuckled. "I can't. They all believe that new-age crap. They wanted to rebury them while Venus is in conjunction with the Sun. End of story."

Al chuckled. "Not quite, I'm afraid. We are going to dig them up. Something funny here."

A big man stuck a gun in his back. "Let's go, Shorty." Harvard cringed. They made Harvard do the digging. He finally hit something. The men yanked Harvard out of the hole, and one of Al's men jumped in and scraped the dirt off the lid. He picked up a bag on top. He opened it.

"It is full of coins boss." He whistled. "It's a bag of gold, boss… wait there are three more bags. The coffin is empty boss."

Al was amazed. "So, how do you explain these, Lieutenant?"

Harvard smiled grimly. "Your men watched us. Let's see, two men, a woman, and a German shepherd were buried alive in the coffin. You dug it up and found four bags of gold. Do the math, Al."

"Already did, Lieutenant." A man knocked him out with a gun butt. They shoved him in the broken coffin, put the lid on, and buried him alive.

The police chief found several of his officers gone. The sergeant was put in charge of the search. He had an idea this was a *Twilight Zone* event, and he wouldn't find them any time soon.

Harvard woke up and crawled down the hole. He heard the gurgle of water. It got loud. The Brady clan saw a frantic Harvard hit the water. He swam towards the shore but saw the blue giants. One of them ate a human foot.

He swam downstream. He saw everyone. Matt waved him towards shore, but the current had him, and he went over the falls into the blue mist.

The blue giants laughed for ten minutes. Doctor Moore appeared with Scott. He was overjoyed to see Sally. He planted a long kiss on a shocked Sadie, "I'm so glad you are okay, Sally." She tried to speak, but he planted another long kiss on her. She saw amused looks on her friends' faces.

Victoria chuckled, "Maybe you should introduce us to your little friend?"

A red-faced Sadie kicked Scott in the shin. "I do not know this person, and my name is *not* Sally." Scott blushed and hobbled off to lick his wound. Sadie sighed. "He was handsome, huh, Victoria?"

They walked down the river and searched for Harvard with no luck. The two girls walked to the cliff edge and peered over. The leader's married daughter apparently still liked Scott and pushed the two girls off the cliff. Larry followed them.

Matt and Brady grabbed the huge girl, but she flicked Brady over too. She picked up a boulder and turned toward Mrs. B. and Matt, who both jumped.

Harvard found himself in a strange bathroom. He was shocked. The shower turned off. The well-endowed District Attorney's wife stepped out. She saw Harvard and *accidentally* dropped her towel. A blushing Harvard bent over and picked it up. She took a step forward, and as Harvard stood up, he found his face between her breasts.

She looked down and noticed the effect she had on Harvard, "My dear husband is gone until Monday." She grabbed his tie and pulled him into her bedroom.

Two hours later, he stumbled out of the house. He could barely walk. He snickered, "No wonder the DA is skinny."

Big Al's men happened to be in his apartment when he walked in. They were shocked to see him. They didn't say a word and just motioned to him to walk.

Big Al's jaw dropped. "How did you dig yourself out of the grave, dickhead?"

Harvard smiled. "I didn't go up I went down through the tunnel to the land of the blue giants... and the *gold*."

Something fell out of Harvard's pocket. "Check it out, boss, they are monogrammed panties."

Al chuckled. "Our dear DA's wife, if I'm not mistaken." Harvard blushed. "Boy, you really get around lieutenant." They drove him to the cemetery and tossed him a shovel. He was too tired from his escapades to dig. Al laughed. "I forgot you were doing the DA's wife, sorry."

Harvard grimaced. "Trust me, she was doing the doing." Two men dug up the grave. The ground had not been disturbed. They found another bag of gold.

Al chuckled. "Okay, hot stuff, back in the hole."

Harvard tried to appear relaxed. "Fine, I'll pick up a few pounds of coins." He tossed them a couple of gold coins he had in his pocket that he got from Victoria. Thanks for digging guys."

Al's men talked to each other. "He didn't get hurt down there, and he was unarmed. Why don't we go, we have guns?"

Al looked down the hole. "Okay, we go. Mickey, you take up the rear. Tie this rope around your waist. I'll do the same. One tug means it is fine to come down. Two tugs pull me up, and we get more men with AKs." If I can't get out, you and Jimmy go for help."

Mickey smiled. "Good plan, boss."

The side of the river was filled with laughter as Harvard tumbled into the water again. He saw the doctor. Harvard yelled. "Bad men come with guns." He then plunged over the falls. The doctor warned the leader. He had his men armed with spears on the shore.

Eight armed men tumbled out of the cave and hit the water. Mickey realized he could not swim, so he pulled on the rope to stay afloat. It yanked Big Al down through the tunnel.

Al panicked and cut the rope to Mickey. Big Al had a second rope tied to a tree in case he had to get out of the hole. He felt weird. Jimmy started to pull him back up. Al was lighter than he thought. He was shocked to find a skeleton with Al's clothes on it. A mighty feast would occur that night.

Meanwhile, to Harvard's horror, he found himself in the DA's bathroom again. The shower water turned off, and his wife stepped out. She was surprised. She giggled. "You animal. We can only do it for four hours. I need my beauty sleep."

Harvard crawled out on his hands and knees. He got home and collapsed facedown on his bed. He groaned; facedown was a mistake.

There were loud knocks at Harvard's door. He ignored them, but they persisted. He finally got up and threw on a robe. He opened his door and saw at least fifty reporters.

A woman pushed a mic in his face. "The autopsy doctor said you bribed him to push out the autopsy for a week. Do you deny it?"

Harvard started to talk, but his robe slipped open exposing the monogrammed panties he must have thrown on by accident in the dark the night before. Several reporters chuckled and wrote down the letters. He sighed. "I will hold a press conference after I shower and have a coffee."

The woman smiled. "And put on a fresh pair of panties?"

Harvard smiled, "Exactly." He would have to think up something good. He burned the panties in the fireplace.

Sadie and Victoria got up off the hot sand. A happy Larry licked their faces. He had a canteen around his neck of ice-cold water. Sadie laughed. "I think I love you, Larry."

They heard a wagon and hid in the rocks. There were two wagons with two male drivers and a leader out in front and two men on horseback. There was a girl with a head wound in the first wagon with a dirty-faced man who lifted the young girl's dress with his gun barrel. She kicked him. He laughed and slapped her.

The girls were shocked when Larry growled and charged the wagon. Larry knocked the man off the wagon but got fatally shot by the leader. The men continued after they took the dead man's gun and canteen. A man on horseback cackled. "Stone told you to leave the girl alone."

Sadie comforted Victoria. She patted her back.

"I'm okay, Sadie."

"Who is Sadie? I'm Sally, you know that." Victoria got a good look at the girl in the wagon. She was identical to Sadie, but she heard the leader call her Abby.

The girls decided to follow the wagons. They reached a vast volcanic glass outcrop. It was called Black Rock. The area beyond was an Indian holy ground. Stone chuckled. "We are safe from the Apache now. They won't set foot in here. We will rest and look for a cave tomorrow."

Victoria and Sally went back to bury Larry, but he was gone. They heard several gunshots from the wagon camp. The leader had shot his men while they slept. The girl, Abby, was not shot. The leader tied her to a dead tree stump for the night.

The next morning, Stone drove the first wagon with all the weapons. Abby followed in the second. He looked for something. He marked their trail. He chipped off chunks of weathered brown sandstone exposing the fresh red sandstone.

He saw Abby throwing out pieces of smooth black volcanic glass. He chuckled. "It will do you no good, Abby." His smile said it all. He would kill her.

They found a large cave. Stone chuckled as he removed the horses from the wagons. Abby knew he was about to kill her, so she hid the leftover dynamite from the robbery behind some rocks inside the entrance. Stone came in minutes later and shot her. He went outside to brush out the wagon tracks with a mesquite branch.

Victoria was shocked to see Sally sprint towards the cave. Stone saw her and laughed. "I don't know who you are, but you're dead." He shot her in the shoulder, but she made it to the cave in time to see Abby light a fuse. A surprised Abby smiled at Sally. It was a strange smile.

Abby threw coins from the bank box. Stone ran in and swore. "Can't you die like a normal person?" He sprayed their wagon with bullets. They both had seconds left. They held hands. Stone smelled the fuse. He sprinted out the entrance as the dynamite went off. He was thrown through the air and broke his leg. He hit his head on a sandstone ledge. He walked dead but didn't know it.

Stone heard a rumble and crawled up a rock. A flash flood hit. It washed away all signs of the wagons. Stone chuckled. *They won't find it now.*

Victoria went back to look one more time for Larry. She was dazed by the heat and got bit by a Western Diamondback rattlesnake. She collapsed after twenty minutes and listened to her heart slow down and stop.

The old Apache found her and buried her next to Larry under the petroglyph-inscribed rock.

Big Al's driver, Jimmy sat in a cell. He traded heroin to the Girl Scouts for mint cookies. He offered information about the two dead girls to the assistant DA, for a walk.

The assistant DA took him up on it. He was brought to an interview room. "So, what do you have for me, ace?"

The driver smiled. "I know what happened to the dead girls and who took them."

The assistant DA wanted the DA's job and would frame him if given the chance. He knew the Lancaster police caused the DA's ulcer. He would love to screw them too. "If your info is correct, you get a walk; if not you get the book." The man smiled and nodded.

The ADA held a press conference about new news on the missing girls and police. Meanwhile, Harvard had his ducks in a row. He made sure he wore men's underwear and opened the door. He was shocked to see an empty room.

He got a call from the sergeant. "The ADA invited the press to the cemetery, to show them what Matt and Brady did with the dead girls." Harvard chuckled. "Well, let's go watch the soon-to-be ex-ADA make a fool of himself." They took a police car with the siren and lights on.

The ADA watched Harvard arrive. "Well, look what we have here, the *Keystone Cops* arrived." The two cops walked up the hill. The ADA pushed it further. "My personal investigation found the girls were buried *here*." He pointed at the old grave. "I guarantee it."

Lieutenant Harvard chuckled. "Tell you what, slick, I'll bet my job against yours that the two girls are *not* there."

The man got mad. "How dare you call me 'slick.' I was the assistant DA."

Harvard laughed. "Well, maybe for the next twenty minutes, if they dig slow." Suddenly, three bells started ringing on three of the ancient graves. The ADA panicked. He put his phone to his ear and left in his limo. Harvard took over. "Get six shovels from the maintenance shack. There can't be much air in there." They pried the first coffin lid off and found a live woman. Her hands were tied behind her. Harvard laughed. "At least the ADA was right about the sex." The press snickered.

The next two coffins had Matt and Brady with their hands tied behind them. The press couldn't get enough pictures. Harvard took them directly to Brady's house.

Matt heckled Harvard. "So, tell us what is going on, *surf boy*." Harvard frowned and blushed.

Mrs. B. chuckled. "Wow, I can't wait to hear this."

Harvard sighed. "I went over the falls and thought I was dead. I woke up and heard water. I thought I was still under the falls.

"I realized I was in a bathroom, and the shower was on. It shuts off and out stepped the DA's wife. She smiled at me and accidentally dropped her towel. I bent over to pick it up, and she took a big step forward. I stood up, and my head was stuck between her breasts. She grabbed me by my um... *tie* and dragged me into the bedroom."

He relaxed. "The next morning, I got home and interrupted Big Al's men as they searched my apartment. They threw me into the hole again. Before they did, I convinced them it was safe, and that there was lots of gold around. I saw them all land in the water, except Big Al. I think they were eaten."

Mrs. B. wasn't going to let him off the hook. "So, where did you end up the second time?" He sat quietly, obviously uncomfortable. She laughed, "Again?"

He sighed. "Yes, again."

The Indian watched the blue men take Abby down a hole. They left a dead Sally lying in the cave. The Indian walked through the solid red sandstone rock. He picked up Sally and walked back through. He buried her with Victoria and Larry. He sat with them and chanted until the sun dipped below the horizon. He got up and walked into the desert. He disappeared in the blowing sand.

The DADA also known as the Dirtbag Assistant District Attorney called a press conference and said the DA set him up. He said that he only followed the direct orders of the DA.

The DA read about the case in the Huffington Post. The ADA blamed him for the fiasco. He took the red-eye back to Logan Airport. The next day Harvard sweat bullets in the DA's office. He came in, "I believe these are yours?" He tossed the Harvard University briefs on the desk. Harvard almost fainted on the spot.

The DA laughed. "Relax, I couldn't help myself. We have an open marriage. She has her hundred dalliances, and I have Miss Biggins."

He sighed. "I know nothing of the lost girls. The little prick is trying to blame me for his screw-up. The asshole will use this event to run against me in November."

Harvard relaxed. "Actually, sir, when he started to attack us, we had some FBI friends bug his phones."

The DA grinned. "And?"

Harvard smiled. *"And* it seems Big Al worked for him."

The DA smiled and then looked up. "He doesn't work for him anymore?"

Harvard laughed. "Al is dead, sir, with all his men. They were eaten by blue… they are dead, sir."

The DA laughed. "Is this one of those weird cases the State Police always stick you with?"

"Yes, sir. Captain Brown is at Augusta National, as we speak."

"Whoa… it must be a dangerous one. Just straighten out the girl's situation, and I'll take care of the rest. Take your time. I will be busy with our little friend."

The two girls found themselves in a field. It was humid. Victoria looked at the vegetation. She got a bad feeling. Victoria picked up a leaf that blew against her foot. She shook her head. "That's got it. This is a giant Ginkgo leaf we might be… We have to get out of here, *now*." They were in a dinosaur nest field.

Victoria tore a piece of cloth from her blouse. "I have to cover your eyes. If you scream, we will be eaten. I will lead you. If I squeeze your hand, stop. We have to get into the woods for protection. You have to trust me." The ground started to vibrate. Sally looked scared, but she put on the blindfold.

A giant dinosaur entered the field. Victoria whispered to herself, *Great, they are carnivores. Well, at least they are big and clumsy. You have to love TRex.*

More TRex entered the field. They walked and stopped several times, but the girls were still a hundred yards from the trees. A distant TRex trotted towards them. Victoria tore off the blindfold. Sally screamed, and most of the dinosaurs started after them.

"We will never make it. They are too fast." One got within ten yards when a loud screech stopped them in their tracks. Small velociraptors were after their eggs. They all charged back to protect their nests. The girls got to the trees and scrambled up.

Sally was shaking. She chuckled. "Well, it can't get any worse than that." A huge Pteranodon grabbed them by their clothes and took off towards his nest site in the mountain.

There was smoke in the air from a live volcano. Victoria saw it first. "Oh no." The animal got disoriented by the fumes and lost his grip, and they fell two hundred feet toward the red bubbled lava. They passed out from fright and landed in a haystack. An hour later, the warm sun in their eyes woke them. Victoria smiled. "It's our backyard." The old Indian laughed from his desert.

Mark headed home from a graduation party in a cold torrential rain. He saw a blond boy on the road with a basketball which caused him to swerve off the road into some bushes. He turned to look and saw an out-of-control trailer truck hit the boy. "God, I would have hit it head-on." He walked home and into the house. His parents were overjoyed. "What is going on here? Boy, Dad, I'm lucky to be alive." He told them the story.

His mother whimpered. "It must have been Scott." Her husband looked at the floor and sighed. They told their son the whole story.

Sadie woke up to loud snores. She was shocked to see Sam and Steve. Sadie saw her basket and looked in. She saw a lonely chicken wing. She chuckled. "That figured." The wine wore off, and the three walked back towards town. She thought about her weird dream. Sam looked just like Scott.

Sam rubbed his neck, "I had the strangest dream. Maybe you picked some bad mushrooms."

She snorted. "Maybe Martha picked some bad grapes."

Steve looked at her forehead, "What is that blue thing on your head?"

"I don't know, a tattoo I guess." She showed him a gold coin. "Look at the date, Sam."

The two tired girls struggled in the back door. Everyone was thrilled that they were all right. Larry showered them with kisses. Victoria grabbed his face. "Hey, how did you get here?"

Matt chuckled. "He and the bird strolled in yesterday. The lazy bird rode on Larry's back." The friends spent the next two hours telling their stories to each other. Harvard's encounter with the DA's wife got a lot of laughs.

Snowflake, the owl, landed on the rail with a flair. Victoria chuckled. "I gather you two won?" She got one hoot. Everyone clapped. She enjoyed that.

Brady chuckled. "We still have to figure a way to explain the girls alive. Maybe our bridge champ can help?" He got one enthusiastic hoot.

The next morning the happy DA had a press conference. There were reporters everywhere. He played the recorded phone calls. It showed the corruption. The ADA barked orders to Big Al to murder the DA. The assistant ran up. He screamed that the DA was a liar.

A large round shadow covered everyone. The reporters looked up and saw a UFO a hundred feet above them. During the distraction, the ADA fought his way to the podium. He pointed a gun at his superior. A circle of blue light from the UFO surrounded the DA.

The man's bullets were deflected by the beam. He swore and fired up at the saucer. He was killed by a ricochet from his gun.

The two girls were beamed down on either side of the delighted DA. The saucer disappeared instantly.

The DA put an arm around each girl and received a standing ovation from the press… that was a first for him.

The next day Scott followed the raven through the vortex on the hill and headed down to the Brady house. This time, Sally remembered him. She kissed him hard, and Scott turned bright red. He protected himself.

Sally asked, "What's wrong with you?"

Scott chuckled. "Last time I kissed you, you kicked me in the shin."

Sally put her hands on her hips. "You never kissed me. I would have *probably* remembered."

Scott grunted. They walked down the hill. The raven rode on Scott's shoulder, which miffed Sally. They waved goodbye and vanished over the hill. Sally's mother was ecstatic to see them. Sally laughed. "Sorry, I left, mom. Scott didn't know I followed him. Wait till I tell you *this* story.

Scott walked back to the Long's home. Their son, Mark, answered the door. He yelled to his parents. "That is the boy on the road. Wait, I saw you killed."

Scott chuckled. "Well, *obviously* he missed me."

Scott's doppelganger would remain with the Longs and Sally.

The middle Scott returned to the Thorburn's home and his dear sister, Carol. He attended MIT, married the chief's daughter, and became a bestselling sci-fi writer. Carol became an artist and sold Scott book covers at a minor discount.

The group at the Brady's had a quiet night on the porch. They watched the sun go down. Victoria chuckled. "Snowflake told me that Scott was adopted by the Longs and eventually married Sally. Snowflake says I was all three girls and you two gentlemen were there too."

Brady and Matt spilled their beers. Brady got in first. "Wait, which ones were we?" Victoria chuckled and yawned. "Tell you tomorrow, boys…"

THE END

By R E Hamilton

www.ingramcontent.com/pod-product-compliance
Lightning Source LLC
LaVergne TN
LVHW041610070526
838199LV00052B/3068